F. W. H Stansfield

# The Life of General U.S. Grant, the General in Chief of the United States Army

Vol. 1

F. W. H Stansfield

**The Life of General U.S. Grant, the General in Chief of the United States Army**
*Vol. 1*

ISBN/EAN: 9783337416652

Printed in Europe, USA, Canada, Australia, Japan

Cover: Foto ©Raphael Reischuk / pixelio.de

More available books at **www.hansebooks.com**

# THE LIFE

OF

# GEN'L. U. S. GRANT,

## THE GENERAL IN CHIEF

OF

# THE UNITED STATES ARMY,

BY

## F. W. H. STANSFIELD.

" Can't is not in the Dictionary."—*Grant at School.*

———

NEW YORK:
T. R. DAWLEY, PUBLISHER,
Nos. 13 and 15 Park Row.

T. R. Dawley, Steam Book, Job, and Newspaper Printer, Electro-
typer, Stereotyper, and Publisher.—Nos. 13 and 15 Park Row,
New York.

# INTRODUCTION.

War has been characteristic of the whole world in all ages, and each contest has produced its hero and its general. But few great generals have, however, been manifested by those wars. Ancient times certainly brought forth Xerxes, Cyrus, Cæsar, and Alexander; the middle ages Richard Cœur de Leon, and Edward the black prince, and in modern times Napoleon, Washington and Frederick. But although these names are attached to great leaders, yet history records no instance of either of them managing such vast armies, over such an extent of ground as has Ulysses S. Grant, the Commanding General of the United States Army. This little volume is therefore set apart to illustrate the life and services of that General.

New York, 1864,                                 F. W. H.

# THE LIFE

OF

# ULYSSES SIMPSON GRANT.

---

## CHAPTER I.

### GRANT AS A BOY.

*Birth and parentage—His adventures as a schoolboy—How he managed a team—His horse trade—"Never say cant"—The defender of Washington, &c.*

Ulysses Simpson Grant, the commanding general of all the armies of the United States, and principal officer during the great battles of the South-West, during 1862 and 1863, and during the Virginia Campaign of 1864, was born at Mount Pleasant, Clermont County, Ohio, on the 27th day of April, 1822. He is the son of a farmer who had settled in the West during that early period, and who had struggled along—as all new settlers have to do—to keep himself afloat. His mother was formerly Harriet Simpson—hence his second name.

The difficulties of reaching markets to dispose of produce made the life of a farmer at that particular time anything but a money-making one; but still these tillers of the soil were enabled to live well even if they had but few luxuries. The sons of Western farmers, therefore, had to work hard on the farms in the various labors attendant upon the cutting down of the forest and breaking up of the virgin soil ; and in this work the brothers of young Grant were consequently engaged.

The ancestors of U. S. Grant were Scotch and were among the early settlers of America. Two brothers—the father and uncle of the subject of this biography—at first settled near each other; but the uncle removed into Canada, while the father remained in the United States. A friendly feeling, however, still existed between them although they differed upon the subject of loyalty to Great Britain. This became manifest during after life in the training of the children.

An incident is reported of young Grant while yet a child. His father held him in his arms at his cottage door on the anniversary of Independance day in 1823. The child was just able to talk, and was pleased with the excitement around. A boy came along with a loaded pistol in his hand, and asked the father to let him discharge the weapon, to see how the child would stand the report. The pistol was duly fired, and instead of alarming the little fellow, he clapped his hands and appeared to enjoy it. He even seemed anxious, by his simple words, that the boy should fire again, and fire again he did. A by-stander remarked that the infant would one day become a great soldier; and the inadvertent observation has certainly been proved a true prophecy.

During the fall of 1823 the father of Ulysses removed from Mount Pleasant to Georgetown, the capital of Brown County, Ohio. At this time the village was in a crude state; but as it was in the midst of a rich farming district it held out many prospects for industrious and economical farmers. In this village young Grant spent his earlier days, and there he obtained the rudiments of his education at the village school.

Young Grant was considered anything but a smart

scholar—he was rather inclined to be dull ; but he was never known to give up a task if there appeared the slightest chance of conquering it. On one occasion he is said to have been puzzled about the meaning of the word " can't," which one of his fellow scholars had applied to his attempt to learn his lesson.

" You can't do it," said the boy.

" Can't," said Grant, then about ten years of age, " what do you mean by ' can't ?' "

" Well," returned the other, " I mean you can't, and *that* is what I mean."

Grant was puzzled at the definition far more than by the first expression, and he made up his mind that he would find out something about the word. He searched the old dictionary, but the word was not in the volume. He went to his teacher and asked him the meaning of it, as he " did not find it in the dictionary."

The the teacher was pleased with the perseverance of the otherwise considered dull boy ; and readily explained that, as the expression was a corruption of the word " cannot," he was not surprised at his not finding it. Being a practical man, the teacher saw an opportunity of making scholastic capital out of the event, and he at once delivered a short lecture to the pupils, ending with the remark, " if in the course of your future lives, you should be engaged in honorable but laborious duties, and your opponents should say ' you can't do this, or you cant do that,' let your reply be in the words of your fellow scholar Grant,

' Can't is not to be found in the dictionary.' "

During the whole of his life up to the time of writing this biography, Ulysses S. Grant has demonstrated the fact that he has not been able to find the word "can't." When pursuing any given object however difficult, if any one said to him "that can't be done," he would promptly reply, "can't is not in the dictionary," and would continue his pursuit with an eagerness and pertinacity truly remarkable.

While a boy at school Grant's father sent him, on one occasion, to get a log of wood out of the timber-land, and gave him charge of a horse and team to bring the log home. He expected his son would find men enough on the ground to assist him load the cart. On arriving at the spot young Grant found the men all gone ; and yet he did not like to return to his father without the log. It was too heavy for him to lift, and the question how to get the log home became a serious one for the boy. By dint of great personal effort he raised one end of the log until it rested on a stump about the height of the cart. He then backed the cart until it acted as a kind of fulcrum under the log, and thus gradually but surely he worked the log into the cart and brought it home. This ingenuity and perseverance in so young a child, although trifling in itself, certainly gave promise of what the man would be.

On another occasion, Grant was sent, when about twelve years old, to make a horse trade for his father. His father told him to get the horse if possible.

"Offer him," said the old gentleman to his son, "first fifty dollars, then fifty-five, and if he will not take that you may give him sixty dollars for the horse. But bring the beast home."

Off started young Grant full of business. On arriving

at the house of the owner of the horse, he explained his errand, when the seller at once naturally asked,

" What price did your father say you ought to give for the horse ?"

" Father told me," replied the boy, " that I was to offer you first fifty, then fifty-five, and finally sixty dollars for the horse."

Of course the horse was " sixty dollars and no less"

" I supposed so," said young Grant. " But on looking at the animal I am convinced it is not worth more than fifty dollars, and I am willing to give you that, but no more. If you like to let me have the horse, all right; if not, well, I will go without."

Grant was obstinate and finally succeeded; riding home on his fifty dollar horse.

The fact of the two brothers differing on the question of loyalty to Great Britain has before been alluded to, and in their sons this difference was plainly demonstrated. The Canadian Grant had a son named John, who was sent to the same school with Ulysses. These cousins would occasionally get into a discussion on the divine right of kings, and the right of revolution. These arguments were all carried on in good part, each maintaining his own opinion, until one day, the Canadian remarked that he considered Washington " nothing more than a rebel."

" Come, Jack," said Grant " That won't do. You must not call Washington ill names. It is true mother tells me I must not fight; nor will I on my own account. Abuse me as much as you like, but if you abuse Washington, I'll off coat and flog you, if you were ten times my cousin. And then mother may thrash me as much as she pleases."

Jack was obstinate in his assertion, and the consequence was that Grant gave his cousin a thorough beating; although he did not himself escape without a few marks of the contest. When Grant returned home, his mother at once discovered what he had been about.

"So, sir," said she, "in spite of all my warning you have been fighting."

Grant explained to her without addition to or suppression of facts, the whole cause of the trouble. The good mother, determined to have her precepts practiced, prepared to administer to her son the chastisement she had promised, when the boy's father stepped between them, and good-naturedly asked to be heard.

"I tell thee what it is, wife," said he, "the boy does not deserve to be punished. He has only defended—as was his duty—the honor of the name of Washington; and mark me, the boy that will risk punishment in such a cause, will rise to be a great man, and a Christian too.

The appeal of the father had some weight with the mother, and young Ulysses was let off with only a reprimand. In after years the cousins again met and in reviewing their past lives, the Canadian asked Grant if he recollected the event of the school days, and the thrashing he had administered.

"Yes," said Grant, "and I will do it again, if you give me the same provocation."

———

## CHAPTER II.

### GRANT AS A CADET.

*How he entered West Point Military Academy—What he there Learned —How he obtained peace among his Companions—" Company Grant "—His Graduation, &c.*

When Grant had passed from boyhood into that period of life verging toward manhood, he began to wish for something more elevated than the simple life of a farmer. He also desired a better education. But how to get it was the question. He had turned his sixteenth year and yet his prospects were far from being what he desired, and he felt dissatisfied.

On one occasion he was heard to express a desire to enter West Point—the Military Academy of the United States. Some friends of the aspiring youth, being desirous to assist so noble a wish, made known his case to General Thomas H. Hamer, who was then a member of Congress from Ohio. The general inquired relative to the merits of the applicant – his qualifications and wishes. On being told that his merits lay in the determination to rise, and his wishes to succeed, the old general said they were qualifications enough for him, and he should have the cadetship if it could be got. The general succeeded in obtaining the appointment, and young Grant entered the Military academy during the year 1839. Colonel Delafield, now General and Engineer-in-chief of the United States armies, was then Superintendent of the Military Academy.

The young cadet did not display any very great amount of the dashing brilliancy which at that time was characteristic of the West Point cadets. Certain outside polish would carry a student to the head of his class and keep him there until he graduated ; but after he entered the army he would be found far inferior to those who had graduated lower. This has been most remarkably demonstrated during the war of the rebellion ; some who have graduated lower than others at West Point, having risen far above their classmates when in the army.

Cadet Grant went in for solid learning. He never attempted to " cram" himself, merely to pass an examina tion; but what he did learn was retained with the pertinacity of his race. He never forgot what he was thoroughly made acquainted with; and never allowed the word " can't" to stop him if he determined to master anything.

Grant, having submitted to a thorough medical examination as to his fitness to become a soldier, and been approved, was placed in the fourth class of the academy. Here he had to perform the duties similar to those of a private in the army, to learn the manual of arms, and all the tactics of an infantry soldier. As the cadets live in tents during the summer, the duties were laborious. His mind was not neglected, for he had to study French and English grammer, geography—especially of the United States, composition, declamation, rhetoric, mathematics, etc. These studies lasted until the summer of 1840.

It was during this interval that Grant first acquired his notoritey at West point and gained for himself the soubriquet of " Company Grant." As a new comer in the Institution he naturally became the sport of the old hands— his seniors. Several practical jokes were played upon him, and some of a very serious character. He endured them for some time, with but an occasional murmur ; until at last he was determined to put a stop to them at once and for ever. The occasion taken advantage of by Grant was when the cadets were out on a parade. It appears the officer in charge—a fellow cadet, but ranking as captain— played a ridiculous practical joke on young Grant; one that he was determined to resent. Stepping out of the ranks, Grant said :—

"Now, captain, will you drop your rank for a few minutes, and stand up fair and square? If so, we will see who is the best man."

Of course, the captain, for the honor of his courage, had to accept the challenge; and off went jackets, and soon the cadets were engaged. In a short time Grant was victorious—the captain being soundly flogged.

Turning to the next officer in charge, Grant said :—

"It is your turn now, lieutenant, to revenge the captain if you can."

A few minutes decided the contest, and the second officer was placed *hors du combat.* Grant turning to his companions in the line inquired eagerly :—

"Who is next? I want peace; I am willing to fight for it; all the company, if necessary one by one. I have no ill-will against any one ; but I must and will have peace in the future."

A shout soon gave evidence of the appreciation with which his gallant conduct was viewed. He had demonstrated that he possessed the pluck to resist aggression, and his companions needed nothing more to prevent them from playing any further tricks upon him. They eagerly came forward and offered their hands in token of amity.

"You'll do" said the captain, although smarting under his defeat.

"All right, Grant" said his companions "We will not bother you any more. You are a plucky fellow and will make your way."

And amid such remarks Grant retook his place in the line. He made no boast of his success, but was not again troubled with practical jokes; and his companions, in honor of the event, dubbed him with the title of "Company Grant."

During the summer of 1840 Grant passed his examination, and entered the third class. It must be understood that, although a large number of cadets enter the fourth class, a far less number rise to the higher ones—many leaving the institution, as unqualified, after passing their first examination.

While Grant was a member of the third class he was selected as one of the corporals of the batallion. He also entered upon the duties of a cavalry private, which is considered a degree higher than infantry. For sixteen weeks he studied horsemanship, the rest of the time being employed in the study of mathematics, French, drawing, &c., and with his infantry duties. In horsemanship he progressed rapidly, and he is now reputed as fine a rider as any in the service. In his other studies he also progressed—slowly, it is true, but none the less surely—and at the examination of the summer of 1841, he passed readily into the second class.

The studies of the second class were far more arduous and laborious than any he had yet undertaken. During the fall of 1841, the winter of 1841-2, and the spring 1842, he was engaged in the mastery of chemistry, drawing, natural and experimental philosophy, and other sciences, as well as in the practice of horsemanship ; and in the summer months of both 1841 and 1842, he perfected his drill in infantry tactics, and began the study of artillery manœuvres in the field.

While in the second class, young Grant was selected to act as sergeant of cadets. This gave him some knowledge of the metho : of keeping company rolls, orders, and other papers belonging to the command ; and enabled him to acquire a system of order which has since been so valuable to him. At the end of the term he was complimented, and passed his examination with credit.

During July 1842, Cadet Grant entered the first class at West Point, to study those lessons, which are sometimes the most difficult—the proper way to command. After he had been in the class for a short time he was selected as one of the commissioned officers of the batallion. He is reputed never to have abused the power entrusted to him ; and yet to command the respect and obedience of all under him.

The studies attached to the first class are scientific as well as practical. During the colder months of the year, which extends from July 1st to June 30th, he studied civil and military engineering ; and in the spring of 1843 took practical lessons in the field. Nor were these all his studies—ethics ; constitutional, international and military laws; mineralogy ; geology ; and the Spanish language had all to be mastered, to enable him to graduate with honor. He had also to acquire the practical knowledge of the art of gunnery, cavalry tactics and ordnance, and other branches of field service ; and to take his final lessons in horsemanship. In some of these studies Grant

became an adept; but in others he did not succeed as well.
He, however, passed his examination with credit if not
with the first honors; and on the 30th of June, 1863,
graduated about the middle of his class, on the same day
with Generals Franklin, Raynolds, Quinby, Peck, J. J.
Reynolds, Hardie, Augur, C. S. Hamilton, Steele, Ingalls,
Judah, and other officers of lesser degree in the Union
Service; and Generals French and Gardner of the Rebel
army.

When a West Point cadet graduates, it is considered he
is fitted to superintend, or take his part in any and all the
branches of the military service. He is supposed to be
well instructed in the use of the rifled musket; the field
piece—light and heavy; mortar, seige and seacoast guns;
small sword, sabre and bayonet; in the construction of
field works, and in the formation of all the material and
munitions used in war. He is also expected to be well
versed in the sciences and to be thoroughly proficient in
all ordinary education of civillife. He is further taught to
be gentlemanly and a man of honor—hence the phrase,
which is always accepted, "on the honor of a gentleman and a soldier."

Having graduated, it is the duty of a cadet to serve a
a certain time—about four years—in the United States
Army; the country requiring that service as a recompense
for the instruction given him at West Point. During
peace, however, this has not been exacted of all the cadets;
many of them having entered upon civil pursuits almost
as soon as they had left the Academy. Yet they can
hardly be said to have been of no service to the country;
for it was under the direction, care and superintendence of some of our West Point cadets that the mighty lines

of railroad that cross and recross this continent have been constructed; while others have had charge of educational institutions and have even taken high positions in the church.

---

## CHAPTER III.

### GRANT AS A SOLDIER.

*Enters the Army—Services in Missouri, and Texas—the Mexican War, Brevets—Oregon—Promotions—Resignation, &c.*

Grant when he graduated was appointed to the infantry service of the United States Army, with the brevet rank of Second Lieutenant. On the 1st of July 1843, he entered upon his new duties and became attached to the Fourth Regiment of Regulars; and was ordered to the West to keep down the Indians on the Missouri Frontier. He was also engaged in superintending the opening up of that country, then almost a wilderness.

The region of territory north of Mexico, and adjoining the State of Louisiana, having declared its independance of that country, the United States authorities determined to assist the revolutionists by sending an army to the frontier. This naturally led to an advance, and on the 1st of March, 1835, the "Lone Republic of Texas" was annexed to the United States. It may naturally be supposed that this annexation would be resisted by Mexico; and threats were uttered that Texas should be again attached to that country by force of arms. To resist such a movement was the object of the United States Government, at the time when it sent an army into Texas under General Taylor.

For some time an imaginary line had divided the American from the Mexican part of Texas; but after a short interval this became useless—first one side and then the other overstepping their boundary. This naturally led to disputes, quarrels, individual strife, and bloodshed. Thus began the war with Mexico.

The U. S. forces having taken possesson of Corpus Christi, a port of Texas, the place was at once garrisoned; and Grant was stationed there, with a portion of the rigiment to which he was attached. While at this post he received his commission as full Second Lieutenant of Infantry, under date of September 30th, 1845, and he was transferred and attached to the Seventh Regulars. This transfer to another regiment did not, apparently, please Grant, as the official records state that during the following November he was re-transferred to the Fourth Regiment of Regular Infantry, with the rank of Second Lieutenant.

The disputes before spoken of, gradually ripened into a severe struggle, without bringing on actual war, until General Taylor discovered, during the spring of 1846, that a large force of Mexicans was about to cross the Rio Grande, for the purpose of wresting Texas from the grasp of the United States. This decided General Taylor as to his movements; and promptly he prepared to resist the advance of the enemy. In the meantime Fort Brown, a work constructed by the U. S. troops on the American side of the RioGrande, was invested by the Mexicans; and, although gallantly defended, must have fallen, had not General Taylor come to the assistance of the garrison. This movement of the United States forces brought Grant upon his first battle-field.

The battle of Palo Alto took place on May 8th, 1836,

and was the preliminary action which led the repulse of the Mexicans from Texas. The following day witnessed the battle of Resaca de la Palma, and in both of these actions Lieutenant Grant distinguished himself for his bravery. It is true, he gained no brevets, as he was merely a subaltern, and naturally the commander of his company received the honors. He was, however, very well spoken of in the company reports.

The Mexicans were driven across the Rio Grande, Fort Brown was relieved and the guns of that work added to the disorder of the enemy's ranks, as they fled from before the victorious forces of General Taylor. The Americans then advanced up the Rio Grande, and Lieutenant Grant participated in the military operations, assisting in the advance into the Territory of New Leon, Mexico.

Steadily the Americans advanced until they came before Monterey, and the Mexicans made a decisive stand behind strong works. General Taylor was not a man to be held back by armed walls; and in this he has been nobly imitated by the present commanding general of the United States Army. Taylor resolved to drive the enemy from their fortifications, and he made a determined assault upon the place. The city was to be carried by storm, and many a gallant officer bit the dust. Lieutenant Grant nobly did his duty during the assult, leading his section with a gallantry and fearlessness of death that has characterized all his subsequent career. Monterey was finally taken ; and the victory ended the campaign in the northern part of Mexico.

A very interesting incident is told of the young lieutenant's conduct during this campaign. A party of Americans had been hemmed in by a much superior force of Mexicans, in the city of Monterey, and there was every danger, not only of their capture, but of their annihilation. A volunteer was called for to run the gauntlet of the enemy and clear the town, in order to bring succor to the party. Lieutenant Grant offered his services; and as he was reputed to be the best rider in the command his offer was accepted. A fleet horse was procured; and, unhurt, he cut his way through the Mexicans, and reached the ranks of his friends outside the city. In a short time he returned with the desired reinforcements, and the hemmed-in garrison was speedily rescued from their dangerous as well as uncomfortable position.

The declaration of war by the United States Congress, inaugurated a more decisive system of warfare in Mexico, and General Scott was placed in chief command of the army. The base of operations was changed from Texas and the Rio Grande to the Gulf of Mexico, and the more northern movement was to some extent abandoned. General Scott effected a landing in Mexico above Vera Cruz, and the majority of the Rio Grande forces were transfered to the command of that officer. The regiment in which Lieutenant Grant served formed part of the forces thus removed, and he participated in the siege operations under which Vera Cruz was finally surrendered on March 29th, 1849.

Lieutenant Grant, heretofore kept in the background by his position, began now to enter upon a new career. It was discovered that he possessed talents of more than the ordinary kind, and he was, during April, 1847, selected to act as quartermaster of his regiment. To supply a regiment in a strange country, with the enemy on every side,

was a duty of no mean importance ; and in choosing Grant
for that office, showed an appreciation, by his seniors, of
his power to perform the duties belonging thereto. With
this position he served through the remainder of the war,
although he did not confine himself entirely to the routine
of that part of the service—his brave disposition requiring
him, at times, to take part in the more serious operations
of the campaign. The duties of the quartermaster's de
partment did not call upon him to enter into the actual
strife; but when Grant found his services could be made
valuable in the field, he never hesitated to give them to
the country even at the risk of his life.

The next battle in which Grant took a prominent part
was at El Molino del Rey, on the 8th of September 1847.
Here he fought with a marked gallantry, and was promoted
on the field to the rank of first lieutenant of infantry, to
date from the day of that battle. Congress wished merely to confer a brevet upon him for that battle ; but he de-
clined it on special grounds.

At the battle of Chapultepec on September 13, 1847,
Grant again distinguished himself by his gallantly
With a few men of the Fourth United States Infantry he
succeeded, after a strong resistance, in carrying a strong
field work of the enemy, and also in turning their right
wing. The conflict was short but sharp. The men succeeded in mounting a howitzer on the top the convent,
and under the direction of Lieutenant Grant the enemy
was considerably annoyed during the conflict. The brilliant conduct of Grant called forth high eulogisms from
all his senior officers in their official reports.

During the subsequent contests, which finally resulted in

the capture of the city of Mexico, Lieutenant Grant continued to manifest that high order of gallantry which had
characterized all his operations from the commencement of
the campaign.

When the congress of the United States met in session
in the winter of 1849-50, the President sent in the name
of Ulyses S. Grant for promotion to the rank of First
Lieutenant of infantry to date from September 16th, 1847,
with brevets of First Lieutenant and Captain to date
from September 8th and 13th, respectively, for gallant
and meritorious conduct at El Molino del Rey and Chapultepec. During the executive session of 1850 these appoint-
ments were all duly confirmed.

After the war in Mexico had been concluded and the
troops withdrawn, Lieutenant Grant returned to New
York with the remnant of the gallant regiment to which
he belonged. For a time it remained as a garrison for the
Northern defences, with the object of recruiting its strength
and numbers, as well as resting from the fatigues of an arduous campaign in a sickly country.

The regiment having again become somewhat increased
in strength and vigor, and the gold fever having made it
necessary that troops should be dispatched to the auriferous
regions to preserve order, keep down the Indians, and prevent bloodshed among the lawless settlers, the Fourth
Regiment of United States Infantry was ordered to the
Pacific coast for the purpose. A portion of the Regiment
was stationed in California, and the remainder in Oregon.
In this latter battallion, Brevet Captain Grant continued
his service, and for a time the headquarters of the command dwere located at Fort Dallas, one of the important

posts in that territory.  From this and the many other military posts, the troops would occasionally sally forth on excursions against the Indians, and in more than one encounter Grant displayed a brilliancy which has since been developed in a form far more valuable to the country.

While serving in Oregon a vacancy existed in the command of one of the companies of his regiment, and Grant was selected to fill it with the rank of Captain of Infantry to date from August 1st, 1853.  This promotion was confirmed during the session of Congress of 1853-4.

A change in the military departments of the United States caused Captain Grant and his command to be attached to the Department of the West, which at that time embraced all the country from the Missouri River to the Pacific.  Captain Grant, who had been for some time a married man,* having become of the opinion that he had rendered sufficient service to the United States to repay them for the education he had obtained from them, and the country being at that time in perfect peace with all the world, determined to resign the service and devote himself to a more settled life.  He therefore tendered his resignation to the War Department, and on July 31st, 1854, it was accepted, and Captain Grant left his military station and commenced the life of a farmer.

---

* Grant married the daughter of Mr. F. Dent, a resident of Missouri, and a man highly esteemed in his immediate neighborhood.

## CHAPTER IV.

### GRANT AS A FARMER AND TANNER.

*Grant on his farm.—The cord-wood dealer.—Collector of debts.—Engaged in the leather trade, &c.*

The retired captain now commenced a new and far different career, and settled upon a farm in the vicinity of St. Louis, Mo. He having had some experience, during his youth, in the management of a farm, he succeeded pretty fairly with his crops; but did not make a fortune or even save money.

As the winter months of that part of the country are generally very severe, and the ground covered with snow for several weeks, Grant employed himself in felling the timber and cutting it into cord-wood. When sleighing was good he would load his sleigh—rough and rudely made—and drive his team with the load of cord-wood to the markets at Carondelet, where he would himself sell the wood to the purchaser. Many a load of wood has been purchased at Carondelet by persons who still remember Grant as a man attired in an old felt hat, a rough blouse coat, and his pants carelessly tucked into his boots. His appearance was then far less that of a soldier than of a sturdy, honest woodman—one who gained his living more by the sweat of his brow than the exercise of his brain.

Grant's mode of living while on his farm was frugal and hardy. He never indulged in expensive habits or pleasures; his wants, apparently being of the most simple character. And yet in spite of his frugality he did not succeed at farming—at least, he "made no money." He was noted for his honorable character—if he borrowed any-thing, he was sure to repay it even to the smallest frac-tion. . In this retired manner the now hero of his country passed part of his life, quiet and almost unnoticed, until the year 1858.

About this time Grant was employed by some of the mercantile houses in St. Louis to collect the debts then owing to those firms. In this he was not more successful than at farming— perhaps not so much. His great fault lay in believing all that was told him by the debtors. If the individual complained of distress, and an inability to pay, Grant at once, and without question, believed him. It was more than probable that he would not trouble the delinquent again, and thus he was many times imposed upon.

Finding after at time that he was not fitted for a " dun" Grant gave up that employment and began others. He was always engaged at something, and was never known to be idle, yet, strange to say, he did not seem to prosper. But in all his transactions he was noted for his candor and truthfulness, as well as his honesty.

About the year 1859, Grant embarked in a new busi-ness, in the city of Galena, Joe Davies County, Illinois. This city had been the seat of trade for the extreme West ; the traders generally travelling by the Mississippi River to the market. In Galena, therefore, Grant established him-self as a leather merchant, and entered in partnership with his father. The firm succeeded ; at least it was doing a moderately fair business ; and the house became somewhat well-known to the frequenters of the city of Galena.

It is in consequence of his connection with the leather

trade that it is reported of him that " he knew more about tanning leather than of politics" and perhaps there is some ground for this statement, as it is not known that he ever took part, while at Galena, in any political meeting either local or national.

There is an anecdote told of Grant that when he was in Galena, some local politician came to him for his vote. Grant replied that he never troubled himself with elections before the time came and then he voted for the one he thought best fitting for the position, no matter to what party he might belong.

While in Galena, Grant made the acquaintance of a young and enterprising lawyer, named Rawlins, with whom he formed a friendship which has since been more closely maintained. On many occasions have these two now noted characters spent their evenings together in friendly and social intercourse—the lawyer admiring the plain soldier, now transformed into a merchant, and Grant becoming interested in one who had it written, as it were, upon his open face, the character of an honest lawyer and a rising man. Thus the two friends became acquainted, and as commander and principal staff-officer have they since passed through the whole war together.

An anecdote is told of Grant that is somewhat connected with his leather business, that is good enough to be true—even if it should not be so :-

One day while engaged in certain duties at Springfield, Illinois, connected with the mustering of troops, a would-be contractor made a proposition to Grant—finding he had some influence with the State Governor—to obtain for him a contract for the supply of the troops with clothing. The offer was one that, apparently, would be profitable to Grant if he took sides with the contractor ; but on the former inquiring how the latter could undertake such a contract with what appeared to Grant to be an actual loss, the contractor began to explain that it would not be necessary that Grant should examine the quality of the clothing sent in, or if he noticed any defects, that he should say anything about it to the governor. Grant detected the attempt to bribe him into a betrayal of his trust, and shortly after, the contractor moved quickly out of the office, his locomotion being somewhat hurried, owing to the proximity of a square-toed cavalry boot on the foot of the indignant mustering officer.

"There," said Grant, "I wonder whether that fellow will appreciate the leather from the Galena store. I never knew it fail under such circumstances."

It is said the contractor has since tried to injure the reputation of General Grant and to circulate reports of his habits of intoxication ; "for none but an idiot or an inebriate would have refused so favorable an opportunity of making a few thousands," would be his argument.

## CHAPTER V.

### GRANT AS A VOLUNTEER.

*Grant Volunteers—His services Refused—Mustering Officer—How he became Colonel—Transportation of Troops after Grant's Plan—How to Reduce a Mutinous Regiment to Order—Services in Missouri, &c.*

The news of the uprising of the South spread over the whole land, with an electric effect. The North became a unit in the support of the legitimate Government ; but no effort was made to coerce the Southerners, until after they had caused the reduction of Fort Sumter, and the lowering of the United States flag from over one of the national defences. President Lincoln, finding that menaces had been made, relative to the seizure of the National Capital, and that Maryland and Virginia had threatened to secede, thereby placing Washington in the midst of an enemy's country—issued a proclamation calling for seventy-five thousand volunteers for three months, and three hundred thousand volunteers for three years' service, to defend the same. The call was promptly met. Under this call Grant presented himself to Governor Yates, of Illinois, and offered his services. He was introduced and accompanied by a friend of the Governor's and the following dialogue ensued :

"Governor," said the friend, "allow me to introduce to you Mr. Grant, of Galena, formerly a captain in the regular army, and who is now ready to offer his services to you."

"I have already had a number of applications," said the governor "for commissions in the army, from men whom I *must* oblige, and at present I have no vacancies for officers. Besides I do not know Mr. Grant, nor to my knowledge ever heard of him.

"That is true," returned the friend, "he has never made himself prominent in a political way, but as he has been a soldier, and desires to volunteer his services, I thought I would give him an introduction."

"That is right," was the governor's reply. Then turning to Grant in a careless way, he inquired what position he desired in the service—not that he expected to find a vacancy for him.

"Any position will suit me, so that I can serve my country," was Grant's reply.

"How came you to leave the service?" was the governor's inquiry.

"Well," returned Grant, "I was educated at West Point, and graduated—entering the army as brevet second lieutenant. I served in Mexico and gained promotion and two brevets. I then returned to the United States and served in Oregon, when I was again promoted. I had altogether remained in the army eleven years, besides the time I was at the Military Academy, and considering that I had given to the country a fair return for the education I had received, I resigned the service and entered upon civil life. But the country is now in danger, and I am again ready to give my services, and my life, if necessary, in defence of its honor and flag."

The governor replied that he "had no vacancy at present, but would take down his name, so that he might have it if needed." With this poor encouragement Grant left the office of Governor Yates.

A few days after the above conversation had taken place the friend called upon Governor Yates, in his office, and found him perplexed amid a multitude of documents, applications, muster rolls, &c;—in fact his papers presented a perfect chaos. The friend inquired how the Governor succeeded as "Commander-in-chief of the Illinois forces," and whether he was sending many troops to Washington. The Governor replied he was doing his best; but he understood little about the matter and was greatly perplexed. Suddenly he turned to his friend, and said:

"By-the-bye, what has become of that queer looking man

you introduced to me the other day; the army officer I mean?"

" What, Grant?"

" Yes. Do you think he would undertake this duty of mustering in troops? Could he do it?"

" I have no doubt he could do it, and I am sure he is willing to do that or anything else to serve his country, no matter in what capacity."

" Well, send him along here. Perhaps I may be able to find a desk in my office for him."

Grant promptly obeyed the summons; and accepted the position of aide on the Governor's staff, and mustering officer of Illinois forces. In a short time, order was restored, from the chaotic mass of papers; and under Grant's superintendence the quota of Illinois volunteers, in accordance with the three months' call, was speedily filled. In fact, volunteers offered so readily, that the Government had to refuse the services of any more for a less term than two years.

About this time the three years' volunteers were enlisting and were officered by the political friends of the State Governors, without regard to their military qualifications. The consequence was, that after a few weeks of camp life, the officers would tire of their duties; and the men, never having been influenced by rigid discipline, would rebel against the authority of those, who in civil life were often far below them in position and social distinction.

Such a case as this occurred about June, 1861. The Twenty-first Regiment of Illinois Volunteers had been enlisted but not organized. It was composed of a body of fine, noble fellows, who were in camp, truly; but the condition and *morale* of the regiment, as such, was anything but promising. In fact it was in a state of mutiny; and its chief commander—a politician—had no control at all over it. Governor Yates asked Grant what was best to do with it—retain or disband it. Grant did not approve of the plan of dismissing a thousand men in consequence of the inefficiency of their officers. He recommended that a good commander should be placed over the men, and he would be answerable for the result. The Governor asked him if he would accept the command, and restore order. As Grant had placed the mustering office in good working condition and could be spared from its actual superintendence he willingly accepted the offer. He was, therefore, commissioned by Governor Yates as Colonel of the 21st Illinois Volunteer Regiment, with rank dating from June 15th, 1864; and he promptly entered upon the duties of that position.

A change was observed in the regiment within forty hours from the time Colonel Grant assumed the command. Discipline was demanded and enforced; and when the men found they had a soldier, and not a politician, to deal with, they rendered a cheerful obedience to his wishes and commands.

About two days after Grant had taken charge of the regiment, a request was sent to Governor Yates to send a regiment to the Mississippi river, to defend the border of the State from any incursion from the Missouri Rebels. At this time all the means of travel had been taken possession of to transport troops to Washington; and Governor Yates was perplexed how to obey the request. While Grant was in his office, the Governor had been in the habit of referring such matters to him; but he was now absent in camp with his command. At last the Governor resolved to visit Grant in camp, and confer with him on the the troublesome question.

"Governor," said Grant, "why not send my regiment. It is ready for service."

"So soon?" inquired the Governor. "I am glad of that; for I always thought the men were sound. But," continued he, "that will not relieve me of my dilemma. I have not the means of transportation, and the distance is over a hundred miles."

"Leave that to me," replied Grant. "Shall this regiment go? If so, I will provide my own transportation."

"How will you manage that?" inquired the Governor.

"March the men the whole distance."

"But can they do it?"

"Certainly. I shall march at their head; and where I can go they can certainly follow." At least, give me the command to move, and in one hour they shall be on the way."

The order was given and in less than an hour, the regiment was marching out of camp near Springfield, en route for the Mississippi River.

In a few days the regiment was in a new camp at Caseyville, a few miles from the Mississippi River, and nearly opposite St. Louis. The long march had tamed down the turbulent spirits, and made the men, what Grant had prophesied they would be, "good soldiers." A short time longer in camp, and they were deemed fit for actual service in the field. They were therefore sent across the river to protect the railroad running from Hannibal on the Mississippi River to St. Joseph on the Missouri River near the Kansas border. This line was important for the transportation of emigrants and troops; it being a branch of the main through line to the far West.

To enable the troops to become inured to the fatigues of a soldier's life, they were continually marched from one camp to another, until on July 31st, 1861, Colonel Grant was placed in command of the forces at Mexico, a station of the North Missouri Railroad, a line connecting St. Louis with the railroad heretofore guarded by his forces. Shortly after, the command was marched still further south and was stationed at Pilot Knob, Madison County, Missouri, Thence the men marched to Ironton, and Marble Creek, en route to the extreme south-eastern part of Missouri, in which the roving bands of rebels had taken refuge after having been driven from the Northern and Eastern counties.

These movements of troops and small skirmishes occupied Grant until August 23d, 1861. Up to this time there had been no hard fighting in those districts of country occupied by Grant and his regiment, although several severe battles had taken place in different other parts of the State of Missouri.

As it was clearly demonstrated, by the contests that had already taken place, that the rebels did not intend to give up the pretended cause without a struggle, and a severe one, the Government decided to appoint a number of prominent officers to the rank of generals, and to divide the country into military departments and distircts. Among the officers chosen to fill the position of Brigadier-General was Colonel Ulysses S. Grant, and his appointment was confirmed at the extra session of Congress of 1861, with a commission dating from May 17, 1861. There were thirty-four Brigadier-Generals commissioned on the same day ; and in the official army list it is stated that Grant occupied the seventeenth on the lineal roll, sixteen outranking him by priority of confirmation. Such was the position of affairs on August 23d, 1861.

## CHAPTER VI.

### GRANT AS BRIGADIER-GENERAL.

*Commander of forces at Cairo— Occupies the Kentucky shore—Grant's unpretending manners—Fredericktown—Belmont—Extension of command —Reconnoissance in force—Movement upon Fort Henry—Fort Donelson— Grant's immortal words—How Grant became an abstainer, &c.*

General Grant was now in a position to take a large command, and consequently was appointed to one suitable to his rank. A post had been, at the earliest stages of the contest, established at Cairo, a prominent point at the junction of the Ohio and Upper Mississippi rivers and commanding both streams. The position, in a military point of view, was of great importance, and to prevent the rebels taking posession of it, the United States Government had ordered its occupation and fortification by the militia. General Grant was now appointed to take command of the post -the militia having been relieved by the three years volunteers—and his jurisdiction extended across the Mississippi and embraced all the shore lines from Cape Giradeau to New Madrid, Mo., and from the northern border of Alexander County, to Cairo, Ill.

Up to this stage of proceedings Kentucky had been held sacred, at least so far as being occupied by the armed forces of either side. It was considered " neutral ground," and was so declared. The adjoining state, Tennessee, however, seceded, and the rebels had built upon the extreme northern border defensive works to repel the advance of the United States troops. Occasionally the rebels would make movements beyond the dividing line ; but upon receiving a protest from the state authorities of Kentucky would fall back. At last they took possession of Hickman and Columbus, on the Mississippi shore of Kentucky, and fortified them ; which fact was no sooner discovered by General Grant than he immediately crossed his forces to Paducah, and afterwards to Smithland, occupying the former on September 6th, and the latter on September 25th, 1861. Having thus planted himself on the soil of Kentucky, he made proper provision against being forcibly removed therefrom, by establishing garrisons at each of the forenamed places.

When Grant occupied Paducah he issued a proclamation to the inhabitants, informing them that he did not intend to infringe on their legal rights ; but he was determined to hold the place against the enemies of the Government. He took possession of the telegraph office, hospitals. railroad depots, &c., and placed a garrison over the town.

Paducah being situated at the mouth of the Tennessee River, and Smithland at the mouth of the Cumberland River, gave the force occupying those places the command of the entrance of these streams. By this means much of the contraband trade previously carried on with the rebellious states through Kentucky was prevented, and a quantity of arms en to route the enemies of the United States fell into the possession of the Union troops.

General Grant made several reconnoisances down the Mississippi River on steamers, and others into the interior of Kentucky by land ; and during each of these movements skirmishes would take place. His command was now extended to embrace the whole of South-Eastern Missouri, in order that he might have power to provide means for preventing raiding parties, in his rear, when he found himself ready to make an advance. On the 16th of October, 1861, he ordered Colonels Plummer and Carlin with their forces to advance by different routes upon Fredericktown, one of the county seats of South-Eastern Missouri, and on the 21st the rebels were defeated and driven from the place. He also ascertained the position of Jeff Thompson's forces and the rebel camp at Belmont ; and on November 6th, at the head of two brigades, moved from Cairo for that point. He landed near Belmont early · on the morning of November 7th, and moved to the attack. General Cheatham was in command of the rebel camp, and although the enemy made a determined resistance, Grant drove them to and through their camp, and their battery of twelve guns was captured. The camp was then burned, and the baggage, camp equipage, horses and several prisoners taken. The movement was a success, and but for the arrival of fresh rebel troops from Hickman, Columbus, and other points, would have been completely disastrous to the enemy in that part of the country. This reinforcement, however, caused the rebels to greatly outnumber the Union troops, who at the beginning were only 3,000 strong, and Grant had to retire, fighting as he went, to the transports in the river where the embarkation was effected under the guns of the armed vessels.

During the contest, Grant had his horse killed under

him, as did also several of his officers, so hot was the conflict. Taking all the objects of the movement into consid-
eration, Belmont must certainly be recorded as one of the
successes of the war.

Shortly after this General Halleck assumed the command of the Department of Missouri, and began a complete
reorganization of its districts. He placed General Grant
in command of the District of Cairo on December 20th,
1861, and defined its limits as follows:—" To include all
the Southern part of Illinois, that part of Kentucky
west of the Cumberland River, and the counties of Missouri south of Cape Girardeau." Of this new district
General Grant assumed command on December 21st. He
then located his various posts, appointed his staff officers,
and made provision for his future advance. He also organized his new forces and located them at different posts,
in view of proper co-operation when needed.

On the 10th of January, 1862, a part of General Grant's
forces, under the immediate command of General McClernand, landed at Fort Jefferson on the upper Kentucky
shore of the Mississippi River; and the commanding General having organized his remaining forces, under General
Paine and C. F. Smith, at other points along the Ohio
shore, at an equal distance from Cairo, on January 13th,
ordered a general advance to take place the next morning.
The forces marched in a triangle and scouted the country
thoroughly, returning to the starting points on January
20th. During this reconnoissance, General Grant discovered the weakness of the rebel forces in Kentucky, west of
of the Tennessee River, and he at once prepared for an advance on the enemy's defences on the banks of that stream.
By this time a number of gunboats of light draft had been

constructed on the Mississippi river, and had been placed under the command of Commodore (since Admiral) Foote. These gunboats were to assist General Grant in the re-opening of that grand navigable water course, and per-formed their part of the operations with great effect.

At the proper time the troops were withdrawn from Western Kentucky, and some transported to the other side of the Tennessee river, while others were sent back to Cairo. The movements of the latter force were noised abroad, while those of the former were kept secret—their place of rendezvous being at Paducah and Smithland.

On the 2d of February, after dark, General Grant left Cairo for Paducah, and gave orders for a forward move-ment by land. The gunboats under Commodore Foote were ordered to start at a time that would enable them to co-operate with the army at the proper moment.

At half-past eleven on the morning of February 6th, the gunboats presented themselves before Fort Henry, a de-fensive work commanding the Tennessee river on the Northern border of that State. The guns of the boats opened fire upon the works, and after an engagement of two hours and a quarter, the garrison of the fort, finding their retreat cut off by Grant's advancing forces, surren-dered to the navy before the military arrived at the post. Commodore Foote, however, turned the work, armament and prisoners over to General Grant, whose forces at once occupied the position.

After having reduced Fort Henry, the next thing was to gain possession of Fort Donelson, a neighboring work commanding the passage of the Cumberland river. This fortification was much stronger than that of Fort Henry, and better garrisoned—fresh troops having but recently been sent into the defences. The Union forces were therefore organized into three divisions, under Generals McClernand, Smith and Wallace, and were so disposed, that in marching they would be sure to concentrate upon the enemy's works at such positions as to secure a complete investment.

On the morning of February 12th, the forward movement was ordered, and by noon the advance had reached the picket lines of the enemy. Dispositions were made during the night to prevent the escape of the garrison, and on the morning of the 13th the gunboat "Carondelet," with General Grant on board, advanced up the Cumberland river, to within gunshot of the works, for the purpose of drawing the enemy's fire, and giving time to the remainder of the forces to arrive at their proper positions.

On the 14th the gunboats of the fleet moved up the river, and engaged the batteries—the plunging shots from which greatly injured the vessels. The gunboats had to withdraw, and General Grant began to make movements for a complete investment of the rebel works by the military forces.

On the morning of the 15th, the rebels made a sortie from their works upon the right of General Grant's line, and by a sudden attack with superior numbers, drove back that part of his army and captured two batteries of artillery. General Grant, however, soon discovered where his line was weakened, and quickly strengthened it by ordering up fresh troops, and manœuvring others. The rebels were again attacked, and all but three of the guns were taken.

The enemy being reinforced renewed the attack; and while Grant was achieving a success at one point of the line, the rebels were carrying everything before them at another. To those in that part of the field, where the rebels were victorious, the prospect looked blank; but when the evening reports were brought in to General Grant, he seemed to be impressed with the idea that the situation was not as unfavorable as it appeared at first. In fact, he stated that the rebels were " exactly where he wanted them." He then ordered a determined assault to be made on the enemy's position in front of the left of Grant's line, the position to be carried at any sacrifice. The works were carried gallantly, after a desperate struggle, the rebels being driven out at the point of the bayonet, and the " Stars and Stripes " placed over the defences, This success encouraged the troops at other points of the line, and the heights, commanding Fort Donelson were all carried by a storm. When the day ended, the U. S. troops occupied a better position than heretofore. The rebel works were all but invested, and the attacking force slept on their arms.

During the night a part of the rebel garrison fled, and the next morning beheld a flag of truce waving over the rebel works. General Buckner having, been left in command of the post by those generals who had run away, proposed a commission to be appointed in view of settling terms of capitulation; but Grant would listen to " *no other terms than an unconditional surrender* " of the works and garrisons. He concluded his reply with : " I propose to move immediately upon your works." General Buckner did not like the answer; but admitted that he was " compelled to accept the ungenerous and unchilvalrous terms " proposed. Such were the words used in reply to General Grant.

The victory was a glorious one. By the surrender the rebels lost not only General Buckner, but over thirteen thousand other prisoners, three thousand horses, forty-eight field pieces, seventeen heavy guns, twenty thousand stand of small arms and a large quantity of stores, besides 231 killed and 1,007 wounded. The Union loss was 446 killed, 1,735 wounded and 150 prisoners. Two regiments of Tennesseeans numbering nearly fifteen hundred men sent to reinforce the garrison at Fort Doneldson were also taken, without a struggle, they being unaware of the capitulation on the previous day.

The capture of these two forts opened up a water communication through the heart of Tennessee and Kentucky, and enabled the Union troops to advance far into the enemy's territory. The defences at Columbus and Bowling Green were thus rendered valueless, as they had been erected to stop an advance which could not be made by another route without hindrance or opposition. Those works were, therefore, evacuated and afterwards occupied by the Union troops.

The surrender of Fort Donelson took place on February 16th, 1862, and in reward for the brilliancy of the campaign, General Grant was promoted to the rank of Major-General of Volunteers, to date from that day.

Up to this time General Grant had been reputed as a hard drinker, and therefore incapable of command. He was very uncouth and careless in his personal appearance; his dress being thrown upon him and left to fall into its place, rather than being properly adjusted. There was but little of the usual tinsel and peacock finery of the fancy soldier in his appearance and far less of the general. This carelessness doubtless added to the bad influence engendered by the report of his inebriate habits, which, up to this time, may have had some amount of truth in it. Many inducements were brought to bear by his enemies on persons in power to cause his removal and, perhaps, their machinations would have succeeded, had it not been for the advice of Admiral Foote, who had noted the genius of General Grant, and did not like to see such an officer ruined by the use of ardent spirits. He visited the General at Fort Henry, and with the candor of a friend introduced the subject of the evil influence of intemperance in the army. He said, the existence of the nation and the rights of humantity demanded total abstinence, especially on the part of those in command ; and Grant being a man of greater sense than was accredited to him, saw in a moment the depth and importance of the words of the gallant sailor. From that day he resolved to be a strictly abstenious man, and he has kept his resolve and has prospered.

Another incident occurred, which arose from the report of Grant's continuous drinking habit. A Temperance delegation from Illinois visited St. Louis for the purpose of petitioning General Halleck to remove General Grant from command, on account of his reported bad habit, as he " endangered the lives of the troops under his command." General Halleck, however, stated he " was satisfied with General Grant and thought they would also soon be." Before the delegation had left St. Louis the news of the capture of Fort Donelson and thirteen thousand prisoners arrived at headquarters, and General Halleck posted the news himself on the bulletin of the hotel.

" Well," said General Halleck, in the hearing of all assembled in the office of the hotel, " if General Grant is such a drunkard as some persons state, and can yet win such victories as these, I think it is my duty to issue an order at once that any man or woman found sober to-night in the city of St. Louis, shall be put in the guard-house."

It is said many took the hint, and a night of general jollification ensued ; and among the most jovial were the members of the temperance delegation from Illinois.

## CHAPTER VII.

### GRANT AS A MAJOR-GENERAL OF VOLUNTEERS.

*Grant's Command again Extended—Movements through Tennessee— Pittsburg Landing—Grant on Retreating—Commander of a Department— Iuka—Corinth, No. 2—Victory—Vicksburg—Advance of the Winter of 1862 and why it Failed—Arkansas Post—Change of Base—Side Expeditions— Naval Co-operation—Grierson's Expedition—Advance to, and Siege of Vicksburg—Victory and Surrender of the Works—Promotions, &c.*

To enable General Grant to carry out his plans, and to move without infringing upon the limits of another's command, his district was increased to embrace all the country between the Tennessee and Mississippi rivers, from the Ohio to the Mississippi State line, and to include Cairo. His headquarters were located at any point where the commander might be. The change of district—which was now called the District of West Tennessee—enabled him to have the use of the Tennessee River for transportation, and, after the capture of Fort Henry had been effected, a reconnoissance proved that stream to be without obstruction to the head of navigation. Grant therefore laid his plans that his troops should be sent up the Tennessee River, and from a point of landing to march to the capture of Memphis, and of the railroads leading thereto.

Meanwhile a co-operating force under the command of General Buell was marching through Central Kentucky, and with the assistance of the gunboats, that had, by the capture of Fort Donelson, been enabled to pass up the Cumberland river, took possession of Nashville, Tennessee. Part of General Grant's forces had already secured Clarksville, and the Cumberland river was now considered as once more open for United States vessels.

General Buell's forces were now to march through Tennessee to the border, marked by the line of the Tennessee river on the east side of the stream, while General Grant was to advance his forces along the west side of the same water course, both armies to arrive at about the same spot near the head of navigation, at about the same time.

Previous to General Grant's advance, the officers of the regiments under his command presented him with a fine sword, of elaborate workmanship. in appreciation of his skill in the taking of Forts Henry and Donaldson. This presentation took place on March 11, 1862. Meanwhile the advance of his forces had already passed up the Tennessee River to Savannah, his new base of operations.

The enemy at this time had concentrated an army in the Southwest, under Generals A. S. Johnston and Beauregard, with their headquarters at Corinth, Miss. The object of this was to prevent, if possible, the Union troops from gaining the lower Mississippi river by way of Memphis; the navigation from the north having been impeded by the fortification of New Madrid and Island No. 10, near the northwest corner of the Tennessee State line. The troops under General Grant had also concentrated at Savannah, Tenn., and on March 15th, 1862, advanced across the Tennessee river into McNairy County, and struck the railroad leading from Jackson, Tenn.. to Corinth, at a place known as Purdy Station. This delayed the passage of the rebel troops, en route for Corinth, but did not prevent their concentration, the enemy having other lines of transportation. By the 1st of April the rebel force was estimated at forty-five thousand strong at Corinth, with reinforcements en route to swell the numbers to about seventy thousand. Grant's army had crossed the river, and was then in camp at Pittsburg Landing.

On April 2d, 1862, the rebels drove in the Union videttes, and the next day prepared for a general advance upon Grant's camp, which, as before stated, had been located at Pittsburg Landing, nearly opposite Savannah. At this time all the forces under General Grant consisted of but five divisions, much less than fifty thousand men, part of which force was stationed some distance to the north, and not readily to be made available. On the evening of April 4th, the enemy made a reconnoissance in force to discover the exact position of Grant's troops, while at the same time a body of cavalry was sent to prevent the junction of these forces north of Grant's position, with the main army. Both manœuvres succeeded, giving the advantage entirely to the rebels, whose object was to defeat Grant before the co-operating forces under Buell could reach him—the plan of campaign having been made known to the enemy by traitors within the Union lines.

Early on the morning of Sunday, April 6th, the rebels commenced their advance, driving in the Union pickets, while sharpshooters began to pick off the officers. Shortly after the main army of the enemy, in heavy masses, appeared within view of Grant's headquarters, and every disposition was made by the Union troops to receive it.

Steadily, foot by foot, the Union forces resisted the advance, until they were forced back to the river, which cut off all further retreat. The enemy pressed them the more closely, when they saw they were falling back, in the hope of driving them in disorder into the river, but the Union troops, although considerably outnumbered, resisted with a determination worthy of their cause. From nine o'clock in the morning until nightfall, it was a continuous struggle—the rebels engaging right, left and centre at the same time, and with equal impetuosity; but the most severe part of the conflict took place in the afternoon—the rebels hoping to effect a complete defeat of the Union troops before night. The enemy outnumbered the Union forces nearly two to one, and the condition of the latter was a very critical one. Grant instantly saw the position of affairs, and knowing that Buell was making forced marches to reach him, he rode along the front of the lines, and called upon the men to stand firm until the troops under that officer could arrive, for on their firmness depended the issue of the great campaign in the Southwest. The two gunboats in the river were ordered to fire on the enemy, and threw their heavy shells into the advancing ranks, checking the impetuous assault. When night closed Grant's troops still held their position on the west bank of the river, but the rebels slept close on their front.

During the night Buell's troops arrived, and next morning the reinforced Union army, under Grant's directions, recommenced the action. The rebels had to fall back; but still they resisted the contest with great determination and bravery, as they were fully aware that defeat would be a death-blow to their hopes. The struggle was obstinate all the morning; but during the afternoon General Grant finding that the enemy was wavering, ordered a charge across the field of battle, and led the same in person. His courage inspired the troops; and amid a hail, storm of shell and cannister as well as round shot, the gallant soldiers rushed like an avalanche upon the foe, who fled in dismay, and never made another stand. Grant ordered an immediate pursuit, and the disheartened rebels took refuge in their works at Corinth—the pursuing forces picking up stragglers all the way along the route.

During this action the rebels lost their leader and principal general, Albert Sydney Johnston, one of the first generals in their army. General Grant was slightly wounded during the contest, but did not leave the field. The Union loss was estimated at 1,500 killed, and 3,500 wounded, with many prisoners. The rebel loss was much heavier in killed and wounded. Notwithstanding the disparity in the casualties, the victory, was, however with Grant and the War Department awarded him its thanks and the thanks of the nation.

A reconnoissance the next day discovered that the retreat of the rebels had been a disastrous one, and but for their strong cavalry rear guard, must have resulted in a decided rout.

When the battle was over, General Buell, a thorough theoretical soldier, began criticising in a friendly way the impolicy of Grant's having fought a battle with the Tennessee river behind his men; a course of action entirely in opposition to all laid down rules in warfare.

"Where," inquired Buell, "if beaten, could you have retreated, General?"

"I did not mean to be beaten," was Grant's sententious reply.

"But suppose you had been beaten in spite of all your exertions, where could you have retreated?"

"Well, there were the transports to carry the remains of the command across the river."

"But, General," said Buell, "your whole transports could not contain over ten thousand men, and it would have been impossible to make more than one trip in the face of the enemy."

"Well," said Grant, as he lit another cigar, "if I had been beaten, transports for ten thousand men would have been abundant for all that would have been left of us."

It will be remembered that Grant's army was nearly fifty thousand strong, and the remark is characteristic of the man.

General Halleck, shortly after this battle, assumed command in person of the forces in the field; and General Grant assumed command of his immediate troops. The army was at once reorganized, and the forces that had been engaged in the reduction of New Madrid and Island No. 10, were added to the command, which now consisted of sixteen divisions, divided into three armies. Of these forces General Grant commanded one half—eight divisions under the denomination of the "Army of the Tennessee," a name still highly honored in the South-West.

An outcry was now raised by the friends of those who had fallen at Shiloh, and by the enemies of Grant and the North, calling for the removal of that officer on the ground that he had caused a useless slaughter of his men. Even in Congress this feeling had gained ground, and it was furthermore reported, with many assertions of truth, that Grant had in reality failed in the first day's battle at Pittsburg Landing, or Shiloh; A strong effort was even there made to cause his removal. But an advocate arose in the person of Hon. E. B. Washburne, who in the face of the whole House defended the cause of a general in whom he placed implicit faith. The Western governors tried to induce General Halleck to remove him from the field; but that officer, knowing and appreciating his worth, placed him, on May 1st, 1862, in a more important position, that of second in command, or commanding general in the field, allowing him to retain the superintendence of his own forces and district.

A number of reconnoissances were next made along the front of the Union position, after which, on May 11th, a general advance was determined upon, in the direction of Corinth. The rebels resisted the movement, and skirmishes and conflicts naturally ensued, until, on May 17th, a sharp fight ensued on the right of the Union line, at a place known as Russell's House. The desired position was at last secured by the Union troops after a hard fight. A new feature now presented itself. As Corinth had been made a strongly defended fortification it was resolved to approach it with counter works, as it was found impossible to thoroughly invest it. The rebel general, Beauregard, fully understanding what must be the result of such a procedure, now began to withdraw his troops, leaving only enough to defend the position against actual assault, and to make a show of front against the Unionists.

On May 21st a division of General Grant's army of the Tennessee took possession of a ridge north of Philip's

Creek, capturing prisoners, arms, equiments, &c. ; and on the 27th another fight took place further to the right, resulting in the defeat of the enemy. Both those contests were conducted under the direct superintendence of General Grant.

Next day General Grant led three columns of troops to within musket shot of the works at Corinth, his advance being stoutly resisted by the troops left in front of those works. The Union force however pressed forward, constructing works as they advanced, until the remnant of Beauregard's army that had been left behind in Corinth, discovering the inutility of longer holding the defences, withdrew, shortly before midnight on May 29th, leaving them entirely unprotected. The next morning the withdrawal was discovered and the works were at once occupied by the Union troops. The city was taken possession of about eight o'clock in the morning.

It has been a subject of wonder ever since that the enemy should have given up so strong and valuable a position without a more decided struggle, especially after taking such pains to fortify it. An assault would have been very costly to the assailing forces, and a stubborn resistance might have delayed the occupation of the palce for some time longer.

Cavalry expeditions had been sent out for the purpose of cutting off the retreat of some portion of the enemy's forces; but the rebels had obtained too good a start, and on the 9th of June was at least seventy miles from Corinth, and entrenched.

On the 20th of June a part of Grant's army which had been in pursuit of the retreating rebels took possession of Holly Springs, Miss., and destroyed the road leading south to prevent a surprise by the rebels.

General Halleck left the Department of the Mississippi on July 17th 1862, to take command of all the United States armies, his headquarters to be at Washington. This naturally led to the re-construction of his Department; and all the country from the Mississippi river to the western shore of the Tennessee, Cairo, Forts Henry and Donelson, the western shore of the Mississippi river and the northern part of the state of Mississippi was formed into a military district and General Grant made its commander. This section of country was denominated the "District of West Tennessee." Within a month it was made into a separate department under the same name.

Very little fighting occurred in the department from June to September 1863—General Grant being principally engaged in restoring order in the conqured cities, and in the suppression of actual aiding and abetting of the enemy by the rebel sympathizers. A skirmish would, however, take place between the guerillas and the post guards; but in these operations the rebels generally fared the worse, as General Grant had looked after all such positions.

September, however, opened with very important operations by the rebels in the Southwest. General Bragg, at the head of a large force commanded a movement through East Tennessee and Kentucky to the Ohio River, and thus engaged the army acting on the East of the Tennessee River. Meanwhile Grant kept a thorough lookout with his cavalry upon any forces likely to operate west of that stream, and this system of reconnoissance kept him fully aware of the approach of General Price's column. Grant in order to be prepared for action withdrew all his advanced camps to the defences of Corinth, and then began to advance on Price's position at Iuka. Early on the morning of September 18th, the Union troops commenced their march by two routes, the column under General Rosecrans advancing by the south, the other under General Ord, and which Grant accompanied himself, approaching the town from the north, via Brownsville. Had the concentration of the forces been properly effected, Price's army would doubtless have been captured; but owing to the haste with which the troops on the south of the town attacked the enemy, the latter were enabled to escape, not, however, until after a severe contest early on September 19th, during which one third of the Union column was killed or wounded. Price's army was severely crippled, losing as much as 216 left dead on the field, besides the wounded ; but not sufficiently hurt to prevent its retreat. General Grant's object was to have cut off all chances of escape by any route ; but the engagement having been prematurely brought on, prevented his plans from succeeding.

General Grant, finding that General Bragg had reached Kentucky, determined to centralize his headquarters, and locate it at Jackson, Tenn , placing a general commander over the post at Corinth. Price's column, which had retreated from Iuka, by a circuitous route, marched to Ripley, southwest of Corinth, and there concentrated with other forces under Van Dorn and Lovell. The object of this movement was to re-take Corinth, if possible. General Grant, however, kept himself fully aware of the movements of the enemy, and had so disposed of his forces that if the rebels made an attack he would not only be ready to meet it, but administer to them a severe castigation.

The concentrated forces of the rebels began their advance upon October 1st, and on the 4th made a determined and desperate attack upon Corinth. General Grant at once sent reinforcements to that place under General McPherson. The fighting was obstinate, but by noon the rebels were driven from the city, in disorder and chased into the woods. Next morning they were followed up and were pushed rapidly toward the Hatchie River ; but they were then met by the forces under Generals Ord and Hurlburt. The rebels were next driven across the stream, and Grant's troops took possession of the heights. The pursuit was still kept up, and next morning General Grant received a telegram that the enemy was " totally routed, throwing everything away." The repulse was disastrous.

President Lincoln, appreciating the value of this victory, sent to General Grant a letter of thanks and congratulations for the series of brilliant operations performed by his command.

General Grant's department was, on October 16th, further increased and extended so as to embrace Vicksburg, and all the State of Mississippi north of that city. It was denominated the Department of the Tennessee.

Meanwhile General Bragg's rebel forces were holding in their possession all that part of Tennessee west of the city of Nashville. The position thus held was in the adjoining department to that of General Grant, and operations were inaugurated by the Union commander of that department to drive the enemy from the State.

General Grant now prepared his army for a grand movement in the direction of Vicksburg, a strongly fortified position on the Mississippi River, and the principal point at which the rebels prevented the navigation of that great highway. He cut down the baggage trains of his forces, and recruited his strength until it numbered four corps. At the latter end of October he sent forth cavalry parties on reconnoitering expeditions, and on the 4th of November, removed his headquarters to La Grange, near the Mississippi State line, and near Grand Junction. This position enabled him to command communication with all important forces north of him, while it brought him much nearer to his line of operations.

The cavalry were again sent forth, this time as an advance guard, followed by a large body of infantry under General McPherson. The enemy's position along the railroad to the Mississippi State capital was thereby definitely ascertained to be as follows : General Lovell held command of the country north of Holly Springs and General Pemberton the country between there and Jackson, the State capital, with Price as a subordinate. The number of men between Grant and the State capital was estimated at about fifty thousand men of all arms.

General Grant having regulated the working of his department, so as to leave nothing behind him to cause confusion, at once prepared for a winter's campaign against Vicksburg. He first sent a force of cavalry and infantry from the shore of the Mississippi River on a reconnoissance along the line of the Coldwater and Tallahatchie rivers, and an expedition to Garner's station of the railroad leading to Jackson, was inaugurated to destory the bridge and track at that point. The expeditions were pushed forward to Panola, Oakland and Coffeeville, and inflicted a great amount of damage to the roads and railroads. These movements were principally intended as diversions from the main object of the advance.

General Grant, with one of the main columns, started about the same time from Grand Junction on the road to Jackson, and on November 23th, left Davis's Mills for Holly Springs—a cavalry force leading the way. On the 29th the advance passed through Holly Springs arriving near Waterford the next day. On December 2d, the rebels evacuated Abbeville, and the mounted Union troops occupied the place. On the 3d the cavalry occupied Oxford after a series of skirmishes; followed the roads through Water Valley on the 4th, and defeated the rebels in a skirmish near Coffeeville on the 5th. It will thus be seen, that the two forces—from the Mississippi river and Grand Junction—were operating in the same region at the same time, although from different points, thereby creating a perfect panic among the rebel inhabitants.

The rebels tried to divert General Grant's attention from his main movement by operations in his rear, but up to this time had entirely failed. That commander, therefore, about the middle of December, 1862, moved his headquarters from Holly Springs to Oxford, Miss., from which point he intended to advance upon Jackson; but the officer he left in charge of Holly Springs betrayed his trust and surrendered that post, with all its stores and supplies, to the rebels, without even a show of resistance. As this post had been made a depot and semi-base for future operations, it not only prevented any further advance of General Grant's forces, but caused him to retrace his steps and re-establish his headquarters at Holly Springs. This disgraceful surrender defeated the winter campaign, as will be at once seen, and the officer who had allowed the surrender, after an investigation into his conduct, was disgracefully dismissed from the service of the United States.

In conjunction with General Grant's advance was another expedition under General Sherman, which started from Memphis down the Mississippi river to the Yazoo river with the intention of striking at Vicksburg from the north, while General Grant occupied the attention of the rebels at Jackson. Everything went well until the surrender of Holly Springs; but this occurring at a time when it was impossible either to recall General Sherman, or to assist by a diversion, the rebels were enabled to reinforce the garrison at Vicksburg by the very troops Grant had intended to keep in his front, and the result was that General Sherman was, on December 29th, 1862, repulsed with some loss. Thus, by the treachery of one man the winter campaign was rendered unavailing, and hundreds of gallant fellows slain.

The first Vicksburg campaign ended, General Grant next turned his attention toward the western shore of the Mississippi river, which formed part of his department. The rebels had fortified a point of the Arkansas river near its junction with the White river, so as to obstruct the navigation. The fort had been constructed at what was known as the Post of Arkansas, and was well armed and garrisoned. General Sherman proposed a plan by which this work could be taken, and his corps, together with that of General McClernand, was set apart by General Grant to accomplish the work. As General McClernand slightly outranked General Sherman, he took the nominal command of the expedition, which was accompanied by the gunboat fleet under Admiral Porter. On the 10th of January the fleet attacked the forts and silenced the battery. Next morning it re-commenced the attack, and dismounted every gun—eleven in all. The troops attacked the work the land side, and after preliminary operations stormed it at one o'-clock, capturing the fort and garrison, nearly ten thousand prisoners, all the guns, stores, animals and munitions of war, fell into the hands of the Union troops—the commander surrendering to Admiral Porter.

This operation removed a powerful enemy from the rear of Grant, and enabled him to change his base to the west side of the Mississippi river. During the latter part of January his headquarters were established at Young's Point, on the Louisiana shore, preparatory to his grand movement on Vicksburg.

General Grant had certainly fixed upon the plan to be adopted, for the capture of Vicksburg, long before it developed itself; but it was necessary to deceive the enemy as to his real object, in order to carry it out with success. He therefore ordered a number of feints and side expeditions to be entered upon, for the purpose of distracting the attention of the foe from his main movement; and in this he succeeded admirably. Among these expeditions may be mentioned those by way of the Yazoo Pass, Lake Providence, Steele s Bayou, and the Williams Canal—neither of which were ever expected to succeed. They, however, engaged the attention of the rebels, and kept his troops employed, until he was able to make his final grand movement.

The navy also co-operated in these movements and diversions; and by running the batteries and other brilliant operations, spread a perfect reign of terror and anxiety among the rebel residents of that region.

One expedition, however, deserves more especial mention than the others, inasmuch as it was the first successful one of the kind during the war. This was the cavalry expedition under Colonel (since General) Grierson. On the 17th of April 1863, three regiments of cavalry left Lagrange, at two o'clock in the morning, and started southwards, upon a raid through the rebel lines from General Grant's department to that of General Banks. A part of the forces returned; but the main column travelled over eight hundred miles through an enemy's country; succeeded in destroying two locomotives, and about two hundred cars; burned or otherwise injured nine bridges; broke up and destroyed the tracks of three railroads and severed two lines of telegraph wire; destroyed three rebel camps, and as many important mails; burned a tannery; took over a thousand prisoners, and captured over twelve hundred horses; making a destruction of valuable property to an amount equal to four millions of dollars, exclusive of its especial value to the army at that time. Grierson found the rebel defensive lines to be a mere shell which when pierced was all but empty on the inside. This cavalry expedition not only diverted the rebels' attention; but also succeeded in severing their communications, thereby greatly aiding General Grant in his subsequent operations. Several cavalry expeditions were started from other points and were carried out with varied success; that of Colonel Streight's from the army of the Cumberland, proving a failure—he and his whole party being captured.

During the latter part of March and before the departure of Grierson's column, Grant commenced moving his army along the Louisiana shore of the Mississippi River to below the line of Vicksburg, capturing the village of Richmond on March 30th, and then pushing on to New Carthage nearly opposite to Grand Gulf. The march was performed at the worst season of the year for travel, and at a time when the roads were soft and spongy from recent floods. Military stores and ammunition had to be hauled in wagons over these bad roads and many times were drawn by hand, as were also the field pieces, etc.

The main column was thus making its way along until, on the morning of the 28th of April, it arrived at the Mississippi river, opposite Grand Gulf, where it was embarked on the transports which had under the cover of night run by the batteries of Vicksburg for that purpose. Under the protection of the gunboats the troops were moved into the middle of the stream, ready to disembark when the works should be reduced; but in consequence of the strength of the rebel batteries, the troops were unable to effect a landing at any point between Vicksburg and Grand Gulf. It was therefore resolved upon by General

Grant to march his forces further overland, until they had reached a point below the Grand Gulf batteries; and then re-embark and transport them across the river to a point where they might effect a landing. The men were therefore disembarked; and the empty vessels were sent down the stream to run the fire from the batteries, which they successfully passed. On the morning of April 30th, the troops were re-embarked; transported to the other side of the river, and landed on the shore at Bruinsburg, several miles below Vicksburg.

Meanwhile, a feint attempt was to be made by a column under General Sherman, as if to land a force of troops north of Vicksburg by way of the Yazoo River. The landing was effected on April 29th and 30th, in full view of the enemy, who made every demonstration of an intention to resist the movement; but after a great deal of noise and bustle, the troops were re-embarked, General Sherman having received an order from General Grant to hasten and rejoin him at Grand Gulf. Sherman's forces were then carried back to the Louisiana shore where they were disembarked, and marched across the country to a point where they could cross the river to Grand Gulf.

The column under General Grant had during this interval been making rapid progress. After landing at Bruinsburg, it pushed on to the rear of Grand Gulf, and as every man was in light marching order the movements were but slightly impeded.

On the next morning, May 1st, the column met the enemy at Thompson's Hills, thirteen miles from Bruinsburg. After a sharp battle the rebels were defeated with great loss, and the village of Port Gibson was occupied the next morning by the Union troops. General Grant was present during the battle and directed the movements that followed. The rebels had retreated over the Bayou Pierre, and had burned the bridge behind them; but Grant's troops soon followed, and a floating bridge speedily replaced the one destroyed. In the afternoon the enemy was pursued across the stream; the pursuit being so rapid that the rebels were not able to destroy their stores, and after the Union troops had taken possession of these supplies they pushed on to the line of the Black River.

On the 3d of May General Grant entered Grand Gulf which had been evacuated by the enemy, and having made it his headquarters prepared to land his supplies and distribute them among his command. He had also told General Sherman to join him at that point; and it was necessary that he should await his arrival. General Sherman began his passage of the river on May 6th, and before the close of the next day had landed at Grand Gulf all his troops, baggage and supplies.

The retreat of the rebels up to this date had been disastrous in the extreme; General Grant not allowing them any time to recover from their surprise. Having received all the supplies and reinforcements he expected the Union commander determined to move with such rapidity as would leave the enemy no time to recover from any of their defeats before another would be administered; and thereby he expected to cause demoralization and panic among their ranks. Leaving General Sherman at Grand Gulf he removed his headquarters to Hankinson's Ferry, and made certain demonstrations as if he intended to advance upon Vicksburg by the Black River route. On the morning of the 7th the two columns—the 13th and 17th corps—that had been with General Grant were now ordered forward, while the troops under General Sherman—the 15th corps—were to follow as soon as ready. All the ferries of the Black River were closely guarded, and every effort made to mislead the enemy.

The Seventeenth corps was moved on May 7th to Rocky Springs, and the Fifteenth corps occupied the old camp just evacuated. On the 9th the former pushed on to Utica and the 1Cth the Thirteenth corps marched to Five Mile Creek. On the 11th the Fifteenth corps passed the Thirteenth and encamped at Auburn, followed en route by the latter, which took the road to Hall's Ferry at the Black River, arriving at that point in the evening. At

this time the three corps formed an immense line of battle
several miles in extent with a tendency towards the east.
On the same day General Grant severed his connection
with the Grand Gulf,

On the 12th the fighting again commenced. The advance
of the Thirteenth corps drove in the pickets of the enemy
at Hall's Ferry, and after a few hours fighting, without
severe loss, the rebels withdrew. The same day the Fifteenth corps engaged the rebels on Fourteen Mile Creek
near Auburn, and after some sharp fighting the enemy fell
back to Raymond. The Seventeenth corps was, meanwhile,
advancing upon Raymond by another road, and met the
rebels about two miles southwest of that village. A contest ensued in which the enemy was severely beaten and
driven towards Jackson. The Seventeenth corps then
moved northward across the country to Clinton, where it
arrived on May 13th. The Fifteenth corps took the vacated position at Raymond, and both columns thus advanced
upon Jackson in that order, moving on nearly parallel
lines to the same point. As these columns again advanced
the Thirteenth corps took up its position in the rear at
Raymond.

The next morning, May 14th, the Fifteenth and Seventeenth corps commenced their march in a heavy rain storm,
and along miry roads towards Jackson. The troops
" advanced in excellent order, nearly fourteen miles," and
at noon the enemy was met just outside of the city of
Jackson, and ready to dispute Grant's advance. An
engagement ensued, and although the rebels were under
the command of one of their best generals, Joseph E.
Johnston, the plan of battle was so excellent that they
were defeated and driven through the city, which was
occupied by the Union troops on May 14th. General
Grant at once removed his headquarters to that place,
and sent a dispatch to Washington recording the victory.

As soon as the city was occupied, all workshops, railroads, bridges, depots of military supplies, &c., were de-

stroyed ; and this work employed part of the forces during the forenoon of May 15th.

General Grant, having ascertained in Jackson that the rebels had resolved upon a certain plan of action, determined to thwart their designs. General Pemberton, who commanded the rebel forces in Vicksburg, had been ordered by General Johnston to move out of that place and attack Grant's army in the rear, while he engaged it in the front. Grant having defeated Johnston before Pemberton could arrive, had somewhat altered the rebel plan; but still Pemberton was advancing towards Jackson. Grant therefore ordered the Seventeenth corps to retrace its steps to Clinton on the Vicksburg and Jackson railroad, and the Thirteenth corps to march northward from Raymond towards the same line of travel. The Thirteenth corps reached Bolton on the morning of the 15th and captured that place with its garrison. The Seventeenth corps passed through Clinton the same day en route westwardly, and General Grant, the same afternoon, had his headquarters in that village. General Grant always moved with his army ; never hesitating to go to any point where he had ordered his troops.

Next morning the Thirteenth Corps moved towards Edward's Station, closely followed by the Seventeenth Corps. The rebels were met near the place and an engagement ensued, which resulted in the battle of Champion's Hill, on May 16th, and a victory for Grant's army. The enemy retreated across the Black River, with the Union forces in close pursuit. The Fifteenth Corps, which had left Jackson on the morning of the 16th of May, by forced marches reached Bolton on the same day, and next day at noon was at Bridgeport on the Black river. General Grant had provided for the means of crossing that water course, having sent the pontoon train by another route, therefore no delay was experienced by the troops on their arrival at Bridgeport. The rebels, who had fallen back from Champion's Hill, had taken up a strong position on both sides of the Black river, below Bridgeport, and their camps were connected by the railroad bridge across that stream. The river could not be forded at that point, and the spot had been well selected as their camps con'd not easily be turned in the immediate vicinity. The Thirteenth Corps having followed the rebels in their retreat, now attacked them on the eastern shore of the river, and the enemy on the western shore, finding that the other camp must be taken, severed the connection between them by firing the bridge, thus cutting off the retreat of their friends in the hope of delaying Grant's advance. The eastern camp was therefore captured, and all the men taken prisoners, after a spirited engagement on May 17th.

During that night floating bridges were constructed, and over these the Thirteenth and Seventeenth Corps crossed the river, on the direct line to Vicksburg, while the Fifteenth Corps crossed the same stream at Bridgeport. Thus the whole army, notwithstanding their recent battles, were advancing at the same time, in three columns, right, left and centre, in the direction of the fortified city of Vicksburg.

During the advance, the Fifteenth Corps turned aside and took possession of Walnut Hills, thereby opening communication with the Yazoo river, and obtaining a new base of supplies. The enemy occupying the works on these hills, finding Grant in their rear, at once evacuated them, and the Union troops speedily took possession. The Seventeenth Corps then occupied the position vacated by the Fifteenth, and the Thirteenth marched to St. Albans, thus the three corps occupied the ground around Vicksburg, as far as their number would allow.

On May 19th, 1863, Vicksburg was nearly invested. An assault was made on that day by the Fifteenth Corps upon the rebels' outer works, but being unsupported the troops did but little more than secure an advanced position, although the assault was of the most gallant kind. The fight lasted until dark, when the assaulting column was withdrawn to bivouac for the night.

The supplies having been furnished by way of the Yazoo River, the troops were recruited from the fatigues of the previous three weeks, and preparations were made for a vigorous assault upon the defences of the city. The heavy guns opened on May 20th, but elicited no reply ; while, at the same time, the skirmishers were pushed forward to within one hundred and fifty miles of the enemy's works. Skirmishing ensued along the whole line, but no general engagement until the morning of May 22d, when General Grant resolved to make another assault upon the enemy's position.

General Grant gave as one of the reasons why he ordered this assault that he was desirous of securing the place without calling for more forces ; as if he could have done so he might have been able to have carried on a complete campaign in that vicinity before the favorable season ended. He further stated that he was sure that, if repulsed, the men would the more willing work in the trenches, as they would then know the defences could not be taken by storm.

The attack was ordered for ten o'clock on the morning of the 22d, at which hour, under cover of artillery, the men charged upon the works with fixed bayonets. The charge was made along the whole line, General Grant holding a position in the centre where he could have a clear view of nearly the etirne field.

The outer works were breached by the artillery in several places, and slope and ditch were carried at the point of the bayonet. The Union flag was planted on the bastions of several parts of the line, and the assault was a gallant one. But the defences were too strong and far too well planted to be thus taken. One line of works covered another, and when the first was taken the assaulting column found itself under the fire from the inner line. Vicksburg was by nature a strong place, being built on a series of hills or bluffs, facing the river, with rugged ground running inland ; and art, under the direction of very skilful engineers, had made it still stronger, until it was now nearly impregnable.

When the troops found they were repulsed they did not despair of success, but settled themselves down with a determination to reduce the place by means of the spade--that being the plan then settled upon by General Grant.

Under the influence of the less violent though none the less deadly implements of warfare, the parallel gradually but surely approached Vicksburg ; and Pemberton's rebel forces were penned up within the walls built by themselves. The navy by the river and the army in the rear, kept up a continued and vigorous shelling of the place, until the inhabitants had to dig caves and burrow in the ground to save their lives. The supplies to the city were cut off as well as every meas of communication with General Johnston's forces at Canton, and the investment of the city was complete—reinforcements having been sent to Grant for that purpose.

To prevent General Johnston from inflicting any serious disaster upon Grant's working parties, expeditions were sent to the rear to discover his whereabouts. Although oftimes threatening to annihilate the whole of Grants'. army, he always appeared to avoid any engagement even with a small portion of the same ; therefore the seige proceeded steadily but surely. The rebels in Vicksburg had stated that they placed their full reliance in the Lord, and expected Johnston to come to their relief.

General Grant while writing to General Sherman the commander of one of these expeditions—intimated that " as they seemed to place their reliance in the Lord and Joe Johnston, it would be necessary to defeat the latter at least fifteen miles off ;" and gave his orders accordingly.

About the middle of June, 1863, a portion of Grant's army was selected to dig a mine under the rebel works of Vicksburg; and the utmost secrecy was kept as to the movement. On June 25th, the work was complete, the powder deposited, and preparations made to fire the same. At a given signal the match was applied, and one of the forts, with men, cannon, and stores, was blown high in the air. The explosion was a signal for an assault and a general artillery discharge along the whole line; and during the confusion the outer works were taken. General activity was manifested by the troops along the whole of Grant's front, and during that night the troops slept on their arms ready for any emergency.

All that night a vigorous shelling of the city was kept up both by the army and navy; and the enemy was not allowed to rest. The shells were, however, fired with the intention of striking among the ranks of the rebel troops; General Grant having no desire to injure the city proper.

The works of the Union forces had by the end of June, 1863, approached so close to those of the enemy that it became even dangerous to look over the parapet on either side. The bombardment still continued and preparations were made for a grand assault on July 6th. On July 3d, General Pemberton doubtless being aware of the result of such an assault, sent a message to General Grant requesting an armistice with a view of negotioting terms of surrender; but the latter would accept of no other terms than " an unconditional surrender of the city and garrison," although he finally consented to meet General Pemberton on neutral ground and consult with him as to the details. The meeting took place outside of the works of both armies, at three o'clock in the afternoon of July 3d, no decisive arrangement being made, before parting; but subsequent communications in writing, resulted in the garrison being allowed to march out with the honors of war, that is, officers to retain their side arms, and mounted officers one horse each; the men to march out by brigade, with their arms and colors, and stack the same in front of the works; the whole garrison then to be paroled and allowed to depart.

This generosity to the conquered, plainly showed that Grant was not only a great soldier, but had also the heart and feelings of a man. He even allowed the plan of surrender to be carried out without any person to superintend it on his part; wishing to allow the fallen enemy all the courtesy in his power.

Shortly after ten o'clock on the morning of July 4, 1863, the rebel garrison under General Pemberton was surrendered to the Federal authorities, and with it the city of Vicksburg with all its armament and stores. The Union troops then occupied the city; General Grant riding into it with a cigar in his mouth.

The result of the campaign was the defeat of the enemy in five battles outside of Vicksburg, the occupation of Jackson, and the capture of Vicksburg with its garrison and munitions of war. The rebels lost about 37,000 prisoners, among whom were fifteen general officers, and ten thousand killed and wounded, including three generals killed. Arms and munitions of war for sixty thousand men and an immense amount of government property were captured by Grant, while avery large amount was destroyed to prevent it falling into the hands of the Union troops.

The Union loss in the campaign from May 1st to the surrender was but 1,246 killed 7,095 wounded and 537 missing.

The results of the campaign were glorious in the extreme. Ninety siege guns, over a hundred field pieces and nearly forty thousand muskets and rifles were captured in Vicksburg. The quantity of working tools secured were surprising.

For this glorious victory, and for the skill with which he managed the campaign General Grant was promoted to the rank of Major-General of the Regular Army to date from July 4, 1863.

One of " old Abe's good jokes " is said to have originated from this success.

" A committee took it upon themselves to visit the President, and urge the removal of General Grant about the time of his Vicksburg campaign.

"What for?" said Mr. Lincoln.

"Why" replied the busybodies "he drinks too much whisky."

"Ah," rejoined the President," can you tell me where he gets his whisky?"

The committee confessed they could not.

"Because," added Old Abe, with a merry twinkle in his eyes, "if I can find out, I'll send every general in the field a barrel of it."

The committee left.*

Four days after the fall of Vicksburg, Port Hudson surrendered to General Banks— the capture of the former necessitating the fall of the latter. The Mississippi River was now opened from its headwaters to its mouth, and the victory was Grant's.

---

# CHAPTER VIII.

## GRANT AS MAJOR-GENERAL OF REGULARS.

*The pursuit of Joe Johnston—Second capture of Jackson—Movements and reorganization—Further enlarged command—Headquarters at Chattanooga—Lookout Valley—Three days' battles at Chattanooga—How Longstreet was outgeneraled—Honors to the victor, &c.*

As soon as Vicksburg had surrendered General Grant sent all his available forces in pursuit of General Johnston's army. The pursuing column was placed under the command of General Sherman; and on July 6th, the Union troops were below Jackson, where Johnston had made a stand. Gradually General Sherman invested the place until but one avenue of escape remained; and this too would soon have also been cut off had not Johnston left the city in haste under the cover of a sortie. The rebel attack was made during a dense fog; but was firmly resisted. On the night of July 16th, the rear guard of

---

* See Old Abe's Jokes, page 96—Published by Dawley.

the enemy left Jackson by the eastern road, and the Union troops took possession next morning.

The city was then dismantled of everything that could be made of use to the enemy and the army began to rest from their labors.

Meantime General Grant remained at Vicksburg, and was engaged in re-organizing and resting his forces; clearing out the various little garrisons that occupied the small posts around; regulating trade with the conquered States; distributing troops about and forming military districts; and in the performance of other duties incident to his position—the details of which would alone fill a volume.

On August 25th, General Grant visited Memphis, where he was received with great honor and enthusiasm, and was tendered a public dinner. That same evening he left for Vicksburg and after an interview with his district commander at that post, he pushed for New Orleans where he paid a visit to General Banks, and reviewed the troops. During the review of September 4th, being mounted on a strange horse, he was suddenly thrown with great violence to the ground, and severely injured. This was considered a sad calamity, as it had been intended to have invested him with a large command on his return from New Orleans. As it was, the proposed movement of the troops had to be made without him, and resulted in disaster at Chickamauga.

As soon as General Grant was able to travel he left New Orleans; and proceeding by the Mississippi river arrived at Cairo. Meantime General Sherman's command had been ordered to relieve the imperiled garrison at Chattanooga, and was then marching overland toward that city. This march was performed amid the greatest dangers from guerrillas and others operating in front and rear.

General Grant was next about to proceed East; but while en route received a telegram from the Secretary of War to await the arrival of the latter at Indianapolis. It was not long before they met, and after the usual greetings, the Secretary presented General Grant with the President's order authorizing him to take command of the three departments of the Ohio, the Cumberland and the Tennessee, under the title of "the Military Division of the Mississippi," with head quarters in the field. This gave General Grant control over all the country bounded on the north by the Ohio river, on the west by the Mississippi river, on the east by the mountains, with a line to be conquered on the south. On October 18th, while at Louisville, General Grant assumed command of this vast territory and the troops within its limits; and then proceeded by way of Louisville and Nashville to his headquarters at Chattanooga. He had now under him one of the largest military commands in the United States, consisting of four armies, comprising nine corps, or twenty seven divisions of troops, besides all the reserves and recruits at the various camps and outposts.

Although Grant was still laboring under the effects of his injuries, he was too much interested in the affairs of his country and of the departments over which he held command, to stay long idle at Louisville. He had made his plans, and started off to Nashville, where he arrived on October 21st. After a short delay he proceeded to Chattanooga where he arrived on October 23d—seven days after he had assumed the command. He found the military affairs of that city in a very bad condition, and he set about re-organizing the same. He also found the only means of supplying the troops was with wagons over bad roads, the railroad lines and the river being commanded by the rebel guns. Horses were being literally starved to death, and the men were on short rations. Everything was disheartening. But Grant no sooner appeared than, as if by magic, a change was soon effected. He had left directions with the commanders in his rear for expeditions against the raiders; and he personally organized a movement against the forces of the enemy that commanded the approaches by way of the river. To open that route was necessary to enable the supply vessels, which he had ordered up, to reach a point where he could land the supplies and transport them to Chattanooga; and as he had already ordered forward an outside co-operating force, he, on the 25th of October sent another, but smaller body of troops from Chattanooga, for the purpose of clearing the way. The movement was a success, and the valley at the foot of Lookout mountain, was thrown open to the use of Grant's forces; and supplies now came forward rapidly.

Shortly after this had been accomplished President Davis visited the rebel army under General Bragg; and while on Lookout mountain, he expressed a belief that the troops under Grant were in a trap, and must succumb to the superior position of the rebel forces, which occupied all the heights around Chatanooga. General Pemberton, who had learned experience at Vicksburg as to what Grant's soldiers could do, at once dissented from President Davis's opinion; and asserted that any attempt to drive Grant from that valley would end disastrously to the rebel army. Davis thought differently and ordered General Longstreet to make a flank movement into Tennessee, and capture Knoxville, thereby getting into General Grant's rear; when, as Davis argued, General Bragg could make an advance from his position, and crush Grant between the two forces.

The plan was a pretty one; but a fair estimate had not been made of Grant's generalship. As soon as that officer had ascertained that Longstreet was really making the movement, he ordered the commander of the forces, who was watching his advance, to fall back gradually to Knoxville and draw Longstreet so far from Chattanooga that it would be impossible for him to retrace his steps in time to assist Bragg when attacked.

General Bragg had no sooner heard of the rapid forward movement of General Longstreet's forces, than he, conceiving the rebel President's plan to have been a successful one, sent a message to General Grant stating that he thought it would " be prudent for him to remove all non-combatants from the city of Chattanooga;" thereby intimating to that officer his intention of attacking the place. To this General Grant returned no answer; but as soon as Longstreet had been drawn far enough away, he ordered the troops under his immediate command to make an advance. Longstreet was then below Knoxville, which had been extensively fortified and made capable of resisting a heavy assault. On Monday, November 23d, a reconnoissance in force was made from the centre of Grant's army; and before the rebels were aware that the movement was in earnest, the heights of Orchard Knob were in Grant's posession

The next day at daylight, the left of Grant s army had made a movement, and by nightfall the extremity of Mission Ridge was also in Grant's hands.

On the right another force scaled the slopes of Lookout mountain, and from the valley of Lookout creek drove the rebels around the point. Over two hundred prisoners were taken during this operation and the Union troops established themselves high up the mountain side in full view of Chatanooga. This position commanded the river, and steamers could now run up to Chatanooga. By nightfall this height was also in Grant's hands.

All that night the heights, right and left, blazed with the fires of Union troops. During the whole day General Grant had been under fire, riding about superintending the movements of his forces.

At daylight on the 25th the glorious "Stars and Stripes" waved from the extreme point of Lookout mountain—the rebels having fled during the night. The valley of Chatanooga had been abandoned.

During the morning of the 25th the artillery from Wood's redoubt and Orchard Knob opened upon the rebel centre on Mission Ridge; their missiles flying over the heads of General Grant and other officers who were watching their movements in the valley. The headquarters were under fire all day long. On the left the roar of artillery was still to be heard, and the heights were there carried, taken and retaken; but the main assault was to be in the centre. At a given signal the line of battle, two miles in length, pushed forward at that point and carried everything before them. Up the steep sides of the ridge rushed the impetuous soldiery in the advance, and being well supported, the whole line stormed the heights upon which were posted forty pieces of the enemy's artillery. With cheer upon cheer the men rushed upward. Color after color was planted upon the summit, while musket and cannon of the foe poured their deadly contents upon the assaulting column. But on they went, and on the very summit Grant's troops captured a gun which the enemy had vainly attempted to carry off. The rebels fled in disorder, and General Grant went forward and located his headbuarters on the summit of the ridge. The captured artillerp was put into position, and the rebel breastworks were turned upon the enemy, whose army was broken in pieces at that point never to recover. Every assault except one was successful ; and that failure did more to ensure victory than if it had succeeded.

The battle field of Chatanooga was many miles in extent, six miles being along Mission ridge, and many more on Lookout mountain. In three days the whole field was won, and the victorious troops were soon in full pursuit of the retreating columns of the foe.

After the successes of November 25th the Union army was put in motion, in three columns, and taking the roads leading south pushed forward to Ringgold. At the Chickamauga depot, while en route, the Union troops captured about fifty thousand dollars worth of the enemy's stores, besides a pontoon train, two 64 pounder guns, twenty wagons, one hundred and ten thousand rations of corn and corn meal, four hundred gallons of molasses, ammunition, small arms and other valuable army supplies. The depot had been burned by the retreating rebels.

At Pigeon Ridge a slight engagement took place, and shortly after the three columns concentrated, and re-advanced. On Friday morning, November 27th, the rebels were met a short distance beyond Ringgold and another severe contest ensued, after which the enemy fell back to Dalton and the pursuit was withdrawn. General Bragg, finding Grant did not follow him farther, then made a stand, and telegraphed the fact to Richmond.

General Grant had now secured the military triangle which commanded the entrance to the Gulf States, and also held possession of a series of the most fertile valleys in the Southwest.

It must not be forgotten that during this interval, Longstreet's forces held the garrison of Knoxville invested in that city. He did not discover the error he had committed by his march into Tennessee until he heard of Bragg's defeat; and then, being desirous to retrieve in part that disaster, he made an assault upon the defences of Knoxville. The attack upon Fort Saunders took place on November 29th, and was gallantly repulsed.

As soon as the victory of Mission Ridge had been effected, General Grant ordered a portion of his forces, then at Chattanooga, to march instantly for Knoxville. Had this movement been effected Longstreet's column would have been captured or annihilated; but to the surprise of General Grant on returning from following the enemy, he found the troops he had ordered forward still in Chattanooga. Without waiting to give the column that had been engaged in the pursuit any time to rest he ordered it forward to the relief of Knoxville; and on December 3rd, the Union Cavalry arrived at that city, the other forces gathering around on the outside. Longstreet becoming aware of this advance of Grant's troops, raised the siege of Knoxville, and took refuge in the mountain passes of East Tennessee. On December 7th, the telegraph announced the relief of Knoxville.

These victories were considered of such importance to the Union cause, that a day was set apart by the President for thanksgiving and praise to the Divine Creator for his mercies and aid in the accomplishment thereof.

The enemy, up to this time, had pretended in their journals to despise General Grant and his plans; but the grand victory at Chattanooga had undeceived them at a costly price. They had called him a fool, but the rebels had to pay for his folly. When President Lincoln heard that Grant had been styled "a fool" he said he had no objection to a few more of them.

On the assemblage of the United States Congress in December 1863, it was moved that a "medal be struck for General Grant, and a vote of thanks be given to him and the officers of his army" for the glorious series of victories in the Southwest. The resolution was carried unanimously, in both houses; and became the first act of Congress of the session 1863-4.

Another resolution was offered " to revive the grade of Lieutenant-General of the Army"; and after a long debate relative to the power of Congress to appoint the person who should fill that position, the grade was re-established and confirmed by both houses of Congress—the members, in their remarks, giving a strong expression to their belief that only General Grant should receive the appointment.

Religious and other societies tendered to the victor of Donelson, Vicksburg and Chattanooga certificates of honary membership of their bodies, and honors poured down in a shower on the hero. State Legislatures presented their thanks, and the Press advocated his nomination for the Presidency; and on all sides the name of General Grant was received with praise and acclamation.

General Grant having paid a visit to St. Louis to see his sick child, was on January 26th, 1864, tendered a public dinner, at which were present all the military and civic dignitaries of the city. Previous to his going into Missouri General Grant inspected the whole of the Military Division under his charge; and even made a perilous journey through Cumberland Gap, in the winter, to ascertain the feasibility of supplying his troops by that route during the inclement seasons of the year.

The bill appointing a Lieutenant-General of the United States Armies passed the Senate on the last day of February, 1864, and on the first day of March was approved and signed by the President. On that same day the Chief Magistrate nominated Major-General Grant of the United States Army to fill the position never before held in full rank by any other than Washington; and on March 2d, 1864, the Senate in Execution Session confirmed the appointment, General Grant becoming the General-in-chief over all the armies of the United States.

## CHAPTER IX.

### GRANT AS LIEUTENANT-GENERAL.

*He submits his plan of Campaign—President Lincoln's Surprise—Activity of General Grant—Simultaneous movement to be Made—The Virginia Campaign—Wilderness—Spottsylvania—The left flank operation—Coal Harbor—Crossing the James—Petersburg—North and South side Movements—Left Flank Again—Shenandoah Valley Operations, &c.*

As soon as General Grant had been appointed to the rank of Lieutenant-General, and invested with the powers of a General-in-chief, he submitted to the President his plan of campaign for 1864, which was for a simultaneous movement of all the armies of the United States upon the enemy's positions, and for the navy to co-operate at given points, and at stated periods. An advance was to be made upon Atlanta in Georgia by the Armies in the South West comprising " the Military division of the Mississippi;" another to be made up the Shenandoah by the military forces in " the valley;' a third to be by way of Western Virginia upon the railroad leading from Richmond &c. to East Tennessee; a fourth from New Orleans upon Mobile; while the main army in Virginia would march across the Rapahannock in the direction of Richmond, a co-operating force to advance from Fortress Monroe. All these forces although widely separated were to be under the orders of General Grant; but the armies moving immediately upon Richmond, would, in addition, be under his direct personal supervision.

The plan was a gigantic one; and was a source of great surprise to the President and the cabinet. When General Grant had left the council, the President said :

" I am indeed surprised at the magnitude of the plan submitted by General Grant; but what causes me the greatest wonder is his implicit confidence in being able to carry the scheme out in detail."

The plan being settled, the next thing to be done was to carry it into operation. It was necessary that there should be no mistake, therefore General Grant decided to place such officers as he could depend upon in the positions of responsibility. He desired to have at the head of each department, men in whom he could trust; and in several instances succeeded. In the South West at the head of the " Military Division of the Mississippi"—his recent command—he had appointed General W. T. Sherman; at the head of his old army of the Tennessee was placed the late General McPherson ; and General Thomas was selected to lead the army of the Cumberland. In the East he re-organized the armies designed to move on Richmond, placing General Meade over the army of the Potomac with young, energetic officers over the various corps, and selecting General Sheridan to lead his cavalry. He visited the various points of his extensive command—East and West—and having definitely settled on the day that the movement was to commence, returned to the armies in Virginia.

The beginning of May 1864, inaugurated the renewal of active hostilities. Cavalry reconnoissances were sent out in every direction from all the armies. Veteran troops at the various outposts were transferred to what was expected would be the scene of actual strife, and their places

filled with new levies. Every preparation was made for a
systematic movement of all the various commands, and a
thorough and vigorous campaign east, west and south.

Having taken a superficial view of operations under
General Grant's command as General-in-chief, we will
now direct our attention to his movements with the special forces in Virginia.

On the 3d of May, the cavalry moved toward the Rappahannock, and on the 4th crossed that stream, On the
5th and 6th, the battles of the Wilderness were fought,
and had it not been for the generalship of Lieutenant-
General Grant, who speedily called up his reserves and
brought them into the fight on the second day, the contest
would have gone badly for the Union cause. As it was
he changed the fortunes of the day by his presence and
forethought.

During the night the rebels disappeared from Grant's
front, and General Sheridan, who commanded the cavalry,
was ordered to find the enemy's position. He found it,
and on the afternoon of that day, Grant's headquarters
were located south of Chancellorsville, where it remained
during May 8th. Meantime the rebels had taken up position at Spottsylvania, before which the Union troops appeared on May 8th. On that and the next two days the
contest raged with fearful violence —the Union troops attacking and assaulting the works with fearful desperation,
and with some amount of loss. During the engagement of
the 9th the United States lost one of its finest officers, and
General Grant one of his best corps commanders, Major
General Sedgwick.

On May 12th the Second Army Corps of Grant's army
made a brilliant capture at four o'clock in the morning.
Taking advantage of a storm and darkness of the previous
evening the commanding officer managed to change the
position of his troops unobserved by the enemy, and before
daylight pounced upon the rebels, capturing an entire
division, including Major General E. Johnson, two bri-

gade commanders, over two thousand men and about forty cannon.

Meanwhile General Sheridan at the head of his cavalry forces statred on his great cavalry raid to the rear of Lee's rebel army, and on May 10th, turned the enemy's right and got in their rear, where he destroyed from eight to ten miles of railroad, two locomotives, three trains, and a very large quantity of supplies. He also recaptured five hundred men of Grant's army, including two colonels, who had been taken prisoners the previous day.[*]

The enemy had begun to fall back from Grant's immediate front, and all movements were going on well, with the exception of the operations in the Shenandoah Valley, which had been entrusted to a general who had been deemed capable, but who proved himself wholly incapable of performing the task assigned to him. A new commander was therefore placed over the Valley.

For the next few days the armies in Virginia remained somewhat quiet. On the 19th of May the rebels under Ewell attempted to turn the right of the forces before Spottsylvania ; but by a gallant movement of the troops the rebels were not only repulsed but sustained a heavy loss in killed and wounded besides three hundred prisoners.

Meanwhile reinforcements and supplies were sent to General Grant, and the army placed on a splendid war footing to enter on a new campaign. The base of supplies had been well established at Fredericksburg, and everything appeared favorable for the Union cause.

Having thoroughly supplied his army, General Grant cut loose from his base at Fredericksburg in precisely the same manner as he performed that operation from Grand Gulf. He wished to establish a new base ; and having seen that everything was in proper working order, and the supply vessels ordered to the new point of debarkation, he ordered the advance of his forces to commence his fa-

---

* For full particulars of Sheridan's operations see " Larke's Life of General Sheridan," price 25 cents.  T. R. Dawley, Publisher.

mous " left flank movement— " first removing all his sick and wounded to the rear. The first movement took place on May 20th, and shortly after the rebel army also commenced to fall back.

The whole army then began to move by way of Guinea's Station, Bowling Nreen and Milford's Station, a section, however, following the road by way of Stannard's Mill. By this movement the main army, taking the enemy by surprise, succeeded in crossing the Mattapony at Milford, without much opposition, and encamped south of that river. The advance then pushed still further forward, and on the 23d of May, the army moved from its position to the North Anna river—Lee's rebel army following the road along the right of the Union army in order to keep up with the movement. The Fifth and Sixth corps marched by way of Harris' Store to Jericho Ford, where the former succeeded in effecting a crossing and getting a position without opposition. The movement was merely a feint, as the main movement was still farther " to the left."

Shortly after the Fifth corps had taken up its position south of the Anna River, the troops of it were violently attacked by the rebels; but after a short although sharp engagement the rebels were repulsed with great loss to themselves, and at once began to beat a retreat.

Meanwhile Sheridan's cavalry had been operating in the rear of the rebel army, cutting communications and creating a great panic within the rebel lines.

It must not be forgotten that the armies moving from Fortress Munroe had some time before this taken possession of City Point, thus holding a base of operations on the James River. The value of this occupation will be seen in connection with the future movements of the armies acting under Grant's personal command.

On May 24th General Grant's headquarters were located on Mount Carmel. During that day his troops surprised and captured nearly a thousand men without much loss to himself. On that night the advance reached South Anna

river, where another feint was made ; the main army pushing towards Hanover ford of the Pamunky.

The next day Grant had his headquarters at Jericho
Mills, and on the 25th at Quarle's ford ; the advance of his
army still pushing ahead on the left.

On the night of the 26th ,the army that had been making
the feint movement near Jericho ford was withdrawn
across the North Anna river, and moved towards Hanovertown, for the purpose of crossing the Pamunky river.

Next morning a portion of General Sheridan's cavalry
took possession of both Hanovertown and ferry capturing
several prisoners.  During the day the infantry came up,
and on May 28th General Grant from his headquarters at
Magahick Church reported the main army across the Pamunky by noon.

While these movements were going on, the people in the
peaceful North had not forgotten Grant.  A few gentlemen of Delaware purchased from the descendant of Washington the gold medal presented to General Washington
by Congress on the evacuation of Boston by the British,
and the only gold one ever presented to him.  The medal
was purchased with the intention of presenting it to General Grant, and cost these gentlemen over five thousand
dollars.

The army having successfully crossed the Pamunky, occupied a front about three miles south of the river.
Grant meanwhile established his headquarters at Hanovertown, and his cavalry engaged the enemy south of Haine's
store, driving him about a mile.

Another movement was made still further north by
Taylor's ford in the vicinity of Hanover Court House, and
certain operations were carried out to prevent Lee from
returning North by that route should Grant leave the way
uncovered by troops ; and also to draw away his attention from the main movement " on the left."

Meanwhile a portion of the forces, which had been operating on the James river under General Butler, were or-

dered to move to the White House on the Pamunky, and there establish a base of supplies.

The rebels under General Lee now began to make a stand north of the Chickahominy river, south of Tolopatomoy Creek. General Grant therefore established his headquarters at Hawe's shop to meet this rebel movement.

On the evening of May 30th, the enemy crossed over Tolopatomoy Creek and attacked Grant's advance; but were easily repulsed with great slaughter. To relieve the force assailed, a general attack was ordered along the whole line, and the enemy was driven from his entrenched skirmish line, which was at once occupied near Shady Grove Church, and was " sharp cheap and decisive,' leaving a number of prisoners in Grant's hands.

Sheridan's Cavalry had by this time re-joined the main armies and was now operating on the extreme left flank.

General Grant next opened his communication with the White House, and thus gained a third new water base since the commencement of his active campaign. He had said he would fight his way " along that line if it would take all summer," and he had now reached within a few miles of Richmond, with a good base of operations, without leaving the line he had started upon. He had, by his left flank movement, neutralized all the heavy works built by the rebels north of Richmond to stop the advance of a " Yankee Army ;" and he had destroyed all means of Lee's main army again threatening Washington by way of the Rappahannock, at least for some time.

On May 31st, General Sheridan, perceiving a force of rebel cavalry under Fitz Hugh Lee at Cold Harbor, attacked, and after a hard fight routed it, together with a brigade of infantry sent to his support. Sheridan remained in possession of the place and held it until relieved by the infantry.*

Next afternoon, June 1st, the infantry relieved the Cavalry, and a line of battle was established, in which order the five corps now attached to Grant's army pre-

*See " Life of Sheridan " for further particulars, price 25 cents.

pared for active operations. About five o'clock in the evening an attack was made, with spirit, upon the enemy's works, resulting in their being carried on the right of Cold Harbor, and partially carried on the left. Several hundred prisoners were taken by Grant's army during the fight.

During the night the enemy made several attempts to gain the lost works, but failed.

On Tuesday, June 3d, at about half past four o'clock in the morning, General Grant made a severe assault on the enemy's lines, driving the rebels within his entrenchments at all points; but without gaining any decisive advantage. The two armies were at night very near each other—some places only fifty yards apart—and desertions were taking place in large bodies—five hundred and ten Georgian soldiers surrendering as deserters in one body.

A sharp fight of half an hour's duration took place on the evening of June 3d, in consequence of the enemy making an attack upon Grant. The attack was gallantly repulsed.

Next morning the enemy's left wing was found to have been withdrawn during the night. General Grant therefore made certain dispositions for future active movements.

On Monday, June 6th, there was some slight fighting at different points of the line, but no serious engagement. Meanwhile certain operations were being carried out by the new commander in the Shenandoah Valley, and also on the South side of the James River.

General Sheridan was also detached from the main army, and on June 7th left Newcastle on the Pamunky River for a grand expedition to the north of Richmond.

For a few days the army was inactive, except in the preparations for future movements; but on June 1th, this qui t was disturbed, by the orders to march by " the left flank." With the rapidity of movement for which Grant's special troops had always been noted, one corps of his command marched to the White House, where transports were in readiness to transport the men and material around Fortress Monroe to the James River, while the other corps marched east along the northern side of the Chickahominy river, the right crossing at Long Bridge, the left moving by way of New Kent Court House and crossing at Jones' Bridge.

The force on the right made a demonstration as if to advance up the Peninsula; and having thus drawn off the enemy's attention, the main column marched to Charles City Court House en route to the James River, which had already been bridged with pontoon bridges in anticipation of the movement. Over these bridges the army crossed to the South side of the river; General Grant's headquarters being on June the 15th at Wilcox's landing on the north side of the James River, below City Point. Meanwhile the Corps that had gone around by the James River had landed at City Point, and at about one o'clock on the morning of the 15th of June was on the march for Petersburg—General Grant having on the previous day consulted with General Butler, at the latter's headquarters, for a co-operative movement from Point of Rocks.

An attack was made on Petersburg on June 15th, and before night the principal line of outer entrenchments was carried. This line of works was about two miles from the city, and with the works were taken several cannon, prisoners and colors. Next morning the attacking forces were increased.

The rebels at Petersburg had, by this time been reinforced by large bodies of troops from Richmond, Weldon, &c., and when the inner line of works was attacked, it was found to be very strongly defended.

The forces that had been operating on the right of the army, and which had made a demonstration as if to the advance up the Peninsula, became engaged with the rebels near Malvern Hills on June 15th, and after a sharp fight withdrew—having gained the object of detaining that wing of the enemy from joining the forces at Petersburg.

On Friday, June 17th, another line of works was carried; but on attacking the inner line, after making several assaults, the attempt to take the works by storm was abandoned. General Grant therefore ordered the positions then held by the Union troops to be entrenched. During the attack they had advanced to within a mile of the city.

General Grant then began to inaugurate a new system of campaigning; although the carrying out of the plan may be the only new part of the design. About the 20th of June he ordered a brigade of troops to cross to the north side of the James River and taking up a position at Deep Bottom, establish there a post under protection of the gunboats. The main object of this movement was for the purpose of keeping a line across that part of the Peninsula from the James to the York River.

About the same time the rebels made at attack upon the right of General Grant's line; but their movement only resulted in their own repulse.

The rebels also tried to stop the return of General Sheridan's cavalry to General Grant, by making an attack upon the White House, Pamunky River ; but in this they entirely failed, although they felt quite confident of success.

Finding that direct assaults were unavailing on the works before Petersburg, General Grant on June 22d, tried the virtue of the further extension of his left flank movement ; and, under the cover of the North side operations, which were merely feints, he moved three corps of his army still further to the left of his line. During the advance on the left a break of the line took place between two of the Union corps in consequence of the troops not advancing together. The rebels discovering this weak point broke through the Union forces, and struck each corps on the flank. The movement might have been very serious to the Union cause had not Grant immediately perceived the difficulty and strengthened the weak spot by ordering up other troops, thus checking the fury of the rebel onslaught.

In the interim General Sheridan's Cavalry had left the White House to join General Grant, and on the same day, June 24th, was attacked near Jones' Bridge, &c., while crossing from the York to the James River. The attack was repulsed after a sharp fight, and next day Sheridan's Cavalry crossed the James, with his wagon train, cannon, &c. The position at Deep Bottom was also at the time being strengthened and fortified.

The Armies before Petersburg remained comparatively quiet until June 30th, when a demonstration was made by a portion of the line to the White House near that city. The movement resulted in drawing the enemy's fire, after which the corps returned to their old position.

A force of Cavalry meanwhile started on a raid south of Richmond leaving camp on June 22d. During the operations, which lasted several days, sixty miles of railroad, belonging to the enemy, were thoroughly destroyed; the Danville Railroad was greatly injured, and thirty miles of the Southside railroad ruined. All the blacksmith's shops, where the rails might be straightened, and all the mills where scantlings for sleepers could be sawed, were committed to the flames; and during the expedition about four hundred negroes and a large number of horses and mules were brought within Grant's lines. The command returned to General Grant on July the 2d.

About the beginning of July, 1864, the rebels, in order to divert the attention of General Grant from his plans before Petersburg, made an invasion of Maryland, and before they left that State even attacked the defences of Washington. The Lieutenant-General was not to be so diverted, but allowed the enemy to come north of the Potomac; meanwhile, however, sending troops around to the defence of the National Capital.

On July 4th, 1864, a monument was erected just outside the city of Vicksburg, to commemorate forever the surrender of that city to General Grant. The monument is of white marble, surrounded by an iron fence, the whole presenting a neat and rather imposing appearance. It has a square base, upon which stands the main shaft, surmounted by an ornamental ball. The full height of the monument is about twelve feet. On the Western face is the inscription,

SITE OF INTERVIEW
BETWEEN
MAJOR-GENERAL U. S. GRANT, U. S. A.,
AND
GENERAL PEMBERTON,
July 3, 1863.

The armies before Richmond now began to settle down to the quieter mode of attacking fortifications with fortifications; therefore, with the exception of an occasional demonstration from either side, or the periodical cannonading and mortar firing, the fighting for a time had ceased. The reorganization had, however, commenced; and several changes were made among the various commanders. This apparent quiet lasted until about the 25th of July, when an attack was made by the rebels, who had been threatening for a few days previously, upon the position at Deep Bottom. The enemy's assaults were successfully repulsed, and Sheridan's cavalry crossed to the north side of the James River to develope the position of the rebel forces. A corps of additional troops was also sent across, and an advance made upon the enemy's works. The movement was a success, the works and guns of the enemy being captured and held.

The troops on the south side of the James and before Petersburg, amused themselves by vigorously shelling the city during the time the foregoing operations were being performed; and the city was fired in several places.

During the whole month of apparent quietude, miners had been at work, digging a mine, intended to run under the principal rebel fort, and succeeded in their excavations, the mines being ready about the last week in July, 1864.

Six tons of powder were deposited under the fort, and at a given signal, on the morning of the 30th of July, men, mud and material were blown high into the air. An assault was ordered and made; but owing to some misconception of orders was not properly supported, and the whole movement thereby proved a failure with a heavy loss of life. The matter was afterwards referred to a military commission to enquire into the cause of the mishap.

The President also visited General Grant to enquire into the cause of the trouble, and during the interview between them, the next day after the repulse, the General reminded the President of a former conversation in which he had said, " I shall meet with several rebuffs before I get to Richmond, but I shall never be farther away than this, and I shall succeed."

This mishap for a short time delayed further operations in the vicinity of Petersburg, which fact being taken advantage of by the rebels led to another invasion of the border counties of Maryland and Pennsylvania. To obtain proper co-operation in resisting this rebel movement General Grant visited the armies in Maryland and the commanders; after which he organized the whole of the states, embraced in the four departments of Washington, Susquehanna, West Virginia and the Middle Department, into one grand Military Division under General Sheridan.*

At about the same time an army and navy attack was made upon the defences of the harbor of Mobile with great success. The plan of this movement was conceived by General Grant, organized by General Canby, and carried out by Admiral Farragut and General Granger.†

On the 14th of August, another movement was made on the north side of the James River; and before the enemy could resist the sudden attack, their works were captured and held. On the 16th, also the fighting north of the James was very successful, so far as it went; but no decis-

---

* See "Life of Sheridan " for the success of this plan of operations.

† See "Life of Admiral Farragut." T. R. Dawley, Publisher.

ive result was attained.  The rebels were driven back four miles with considerable loss in killed and wounded, besides the capture of over four hundred prisoners.  Two rebel generals were killed, and a large number of wounded prisoners were also captured.

One of the objects of the movement on the north side of the James River was to draw the rebels from Petersburg, so as to uncover the Weldon railroad; and this plan was entirely successful.  On August 18th, the corps on the extreme left moved out and firmly established itself on that road, from which it was not afterwards removed, although the enemy made several severe attacks upon the position thus gained.  The movement was a complete surprise and the Union forces were at once strengthened in their position; and finding Grant's troops could not be driven therefrom, the rebels withdrew and threw up defensive works in their new front.

A part of Grant's forces next extended their left as far as Ream's station, where on August 25th, the enemy attacked several times during the day.  The Union troops repulsed the assault every time, until at about half past five in the evening a fearful assault was made on the centre and left of the Union lines.  The attack was probably intended by the enemy to have been simultaneous, as the rebel forces had formed in the wood, and had placed their artillery in position.  Under cover of a heavy cannonade, lasting for about fifteen minutes, the assault was made; but was firmly resisted.  The fighting was continuous until dark, the enemy being held in check by the artillery, dismounted cavalry and skirmishers of the Union forces.  At dark the garrison was withdrawn, leaving a safeguard behind. The enemy made no further advance that night, and when the safe guard was about to withdraw in the morning they discovered that the enemy had fallen back.

The upper part of the Weldon railroad nearest Petersburg, was, however, still held by the extreme left of Grant's line; and although he had by the withdrawal above described given up the lower part of the road, the line of communication between Petersburg and the south by this route was still severed.

Again the armies before Richmond settled down for a time into comparative quiet; and the troops were employed in cutting a canal at Dutch Gap of the James River, and in building a railroad to connect the extreme left of General Grant's line with his head quarters at City Point. The rebels tried to interfere with these operations by shelling the workmen, but still the work steadily progressed. The labor on the canal was indeed great, and after the war is ended will stand as a monument of engineering skill equal with that which reduced Fort Pulaski, Sumter, Island No. 10, &c., and through which Charleston was shelled from the swamp.

On August 16th, 1854, General Grant wrote his famous letter in which he pointed out the delapidated condition of the South, and their only hope—a divided North and mighty unity of action to secure victory.

About this time Atlanta was taken possession of by General Sherman—the occupation of that city being the grand result of the campaign which had been inaugurated by General Grant before he left the South-West.*

On September 5th a slight movement of the Union forces on the left was made to obtain a better position ; and on September 10th, another movement was made by which a picket line of the enemy was taken and their entrenched position captured entire without scarcely firing a shot.

General Grant on the 15th of September left City Point ostensibly to pay a visit to his family in New Jersey ; but on the way he spent a few hours at the headquarters of General Sheridan. What transpired there is not recorded ; but almost immediately after his departure, General Sheridan commenced in the Shenadoah Valley that vigorous campaign which resulted in the complete destruction of Early's army, and the devastation of the whole region. †

* For details see "Life of Sherman," Price, 25 cents. T. R. Dawley, Publisher.

† See Life of Sheridan.

General Grant after visiting his family returned to his headquarters at City Point on September 19th, only four days from the time he left. Long furloughs are not a portion of General Grant's military routine of personal services.

On the 29th of September, 1864, a movement was made by two corps of Grant's army on the north side of the James River, and the works attacked along their front— one corps carrying the very strong fortification and a long tine of entrenchments below Chapin's farm, capturing fifteen pieces of artillery and a few hundred prisoners; while the other corps carried the New Market entrenchments on the road from Deep Bottom.

When the foregoing operation had been fairly begun, General Grant pushed forward his left flank, carried the line of works along the front, and captured a number of prisoners. Another portion of his forces took possession of the rebel works at Poplar Grove Church, also on the left. To enable him to accomplish these movements on the left was the principal object of the advance north of the James River; for the rebels immediately weakened their lines opposite Grant's left to resist that movement.

About this time General Grant, finding that the inhabitants of the Shenandoah region continued their treacherous depredations and murders on the troops that were actually protecting them and theirs, issued an order to General Sheridan embracing the following words :

" Do all the damage you can to the railroad and crops. Carry off stock of all descriptions and negroes, so as to prevent further planting. If the war is to last another year, let the Shenandoah Valley remain a barren waste." Sheridan carried out the order.

The rebels on October 7th attempted to turn the flank of the right of Grant's army, north of the James, and succeeded in driving in the cavalry outposts, and capturing their guns, following up the same with an attack upon the infantry along the New Market road. The infantry succeeded in repulsing the enemy, and the whole of the attacks were thereby rendered of no avail to the rebel cause.

Cavalry reconnoissances were made at different times, and on October 11th, a force started to scout in the region of the Southside Railroad as far as Stony Creek. This led to a slight engagement and the capture of a few prisoners. With the exception of this, the Armies South of Richmond were comparatively quiet; and the Dutch Gap Canal still progressed.

Meantime General Sheridan fought his grand battles of " Cedar Creek," by which he cleared the Valley, at least for a time, of all the rebel forces therein.

General Grant kept his troops somewhat advanced near Hatcher's Run in the hope of inviting an attack, which was made by the rebels on October 27th ; and in the end the latter were repulsed with some loss. General Grant then drew in his lines to their former position to await further developments.

---

## CHAPTER X.

### GENERAL GRANT'S PERSONAL APPEARANCE.

Those who has never seen General Grant would scarcely be likely to single him out from the hundred others on the ground before Richmond, as the man whom the country recognizes as having done the most, and of whom so much is expected, to crush the rebellion by hard blows, and of the exercise of those qualities which enter into a character of true greatness. He is there generally to be seen enveloped in a rather huge military coat, wearing a slouching hat, which seems to have a predisposition to turn up before and down behind, giving his orders with as few words as possible, in a low tone, and with an accent which partakes of the slight nervousness, intensity of feeling,

yet perfect self-command, seen in all his movements.
General Grant might be described best as a little old
man—yet not really old—who, with a keen eye, does not
intend that anything should escape his observation.  At
the last battle he was not in his usual physical condition,
his recent illness, added to his arduous labors, having
made him lean in flesh, and given a sharpness to his features which he did not formerly have.  Those features,
however, go far to define the man of will and self-control
that he is.  At the critical moment of the day's operations, the muscles seemed to gather tighter and harder
over his slightly projecting chin, which seems to have an
involuntary way of working, and the lips to contract.
There is in what he does or says nothing that has the
slightest approach to ostentation of show, but the palpable
evidence of a plain man of sense, will and purpose, who
has little idea that more eyes are turned on him than on
any other man on the continent.  From his first struggle
at Belmont to his last before Richmond, the men led by
him have fought more steadily, fiercely and successfully
than those of any other portion of our army.  In looking
back over the history of the war, the eye rests upon no
more glorious pages than those whereon are written Fort
Donelson, Vicksburg, and Chattanooga.  He has no host
of flatterers, holds no correspondence with politicians,
never grumbles at President Lincoln or the War Department, does not consider himself a persecuted man, and is
cheerful and content with the position and duties assigned
him.  He never needs to be ordered peremptorily to fight
the enemy, for the plain reason that he is prompt to fight
whenever the occasion offers.  He cultivates no popularity
among the soldiers.  He leaves his deeds to speak for him,
and takes no pains with his reputation.  In fact, he is a
model for all our officers.

FINIS.

# INCIDENTS

OF

# AMERICAN CAMP LIFE

## BEING EVENTS WHICH HAVE ACTUALLY TAKEN PLACE
## DURING THE PRESENT REBELLION.

### CONTENTS :

# MERCEDES:
OR,
# THE OUTLAW'S CHILD
## A Wild and Singular Story.

THE scenes of this strange story are laid in California, commencing some years before the gold mines were discovered, and brought to the time "when mobs and murders were plentiful as golden slugs:" when gamblers were reckoned right and proper men, and gambling hells were the saloons of fashion, and men of mind, manners and money amused themselves therein; when theatres outnumbered churches, and play-books, Bibles; when courtezans were the acknowledged leaders of *ton*; when San Francisco rivaled her elder sisters, both of the Old and New World, in her bowers of pleasure—for here was the great nucleus of splendor and gratification in every sense. Fortunes were made in a single day by men who had made fortunes in the mines came here. What wonder, then, if crime jostled time in the streets. What wonder if fraud throve in the mart of opulence, or that mid night brawls disturbed the repose of the few who tried to be just.

Then arose the Vigilance Committee, taking judgment into their own hands, when th quivering bodies of miscreant offenders, swung from the wide windows of the Committee rooms in Battery Street, an awful example of the doom of evil.

**Price—15 Cents, each number.** Mailed, postpaid, or four copies fo 0 cents.

## T. R. DAWLEY, Publisher,
### 13 and 15 Park Row. New York.

# No. 1.—BALLADS OF THE WAR.

### CONTENTS:

# No. 2.—BALLADS OF THE SOUTH.

### CONTENTS:

Price 10 cts.    T. R. DAWLEY, Publisher, 13 & 15 Park Row, N. Y.

# DAWLEY'S TENPENNY NOVELS, NO. 2.

# DICK DARE-DEVIL;

## OR,

# THE CURSE OF GOLD.

### *A STORY of LAND and SEA.*

This is a most singular story, of a young man who was cursed by the power of gold,—having had an immense fortune placed to his credit in a bank, by a mysterious individual unknown to him ; after which he became associated with gamblers and bad men. by whom he became involved in a duel,—was wounded,—became a wanderer, was impressed into the British Navy, where his career commences as Dick Dare-Devil—a dauntless sailor, and one of the most daring, we might say reckless fighting men in the British Navy, through whose means the " Santissima," a Spanish corvette, was captured, loaded with an amount of doubloons, mordores, and pieces of Eight that would be astonishing even to the people of our own day.

## CONTENTS.

Sold by book-sellers and news-dealers everywhere. Price, Ten cents, post-paid, by mail. T. R, DAWLEY, Publisher, 13 & 15 Park

www.ingramcontent.com/pod-product-compliance
Lightning Source LLC
Chambersburg PA
CBHW032205010726
47493CB00008BA/2832